the 310:
LIFE AS A POSER

# the 310:
# LIFE AS A POSER
## beth killian

POCKET BOOKS    MTV BOOKS

New York  London  Toronto  Sydney

POCKET BOOKS, a division of Simon & Schuster, Inc.
1230 Avenue of the Americas, New York, NY 10020

ISBN-13: 978-1-4165-2031-3
ISBN-10:    1-4165-2031-7

This MTV Books/Pocket Books trade paperback edition March 2006

10  9  8  7  6  5  4  3  2  1

Manufactured in the United States of America

For information regarding special discounts for bulk purchases,
please contact Simon & Schuster Special Sales at 1-800-456-6798 or
business@simonandschuster.com.

For Amy,
the coolest chick in the 212

the 310:
# LIFE AS A POSER

From: OutOfEden@globecon.com <eva cordes>
To: descartesismybizatch@wordup.net <Jeff Oerte>
Subject: WTF?
WTF? I can't believe you wouldn't even say good-bye.
We've known each other since you forced me to eat paste
in kindergarten and you can't choke out a "bon voyage"?
That's cold, dude. Cold.
Will you please write me back? Finally??? I SAID I WAS
SORRY.
Don't make me beg. I ate paste for you.
E.

From: descartesismybizatch@wordup.net <Jeff Oerte>
To: OutOfEden@globecon.com <eva cordes>
Subject: RE: WTF?
If you didn't want to hang out with me, you should have
just said something. You didn't have to freak Bryan
"Smegma Boy" Dufort in front of the whole school. I can
take a hint.
Jeff
P.S. The girl who moved into your grandparents' house is
blonde and hot and has a ***total*** weakness for mathe-
matically gifted, Dartmouth-bound pasty boys.

# 1

I felt sure that my life had changed for the better before we even landed in Los Angeles—but then, *everything* seems better in first class.

I'd gotten bumped up from coach courtesy of my Aunt Laurel, who had called the airline and forked over some of her frequent flyer miles. "Evie, pet, I have five and a half billion extra miles—the least I can do is get you out of steerage." That's what she'd said, and of course I'd gushed with gratitude.

But I don't think she really did it out of some belated sense of auntly adoration. I think she did it because she felt guilty about dumping me with my grandparents for the past fourteen years. And also because she didn't want me picking up any nasty colds or sore throats in economy class and getting her sick. "Don't forget your Emer'gen-C before takeoff," was how she'd closed every phone conversation for the past two weeks.

But whatever—who cares why she did it because the bottom line is, first class *rocks*. I'd never been on the other side of the curtain on an airplane, and now I knew what I'd been missing all these years: Lemon-scented hot towels! A three-course meal with real silverware and linen napkins! Warm chocolate chip cookies straight out of the oven! The flight attendants fawned all over me like I was Beyoncé and they were the entourage, despite the fact that I was wearing a ratty sweatshirt and comfy jeans that were a wee bit overdue for a wash. (However, they were shockingly stubborn in their refusal to dispense any of the complimentary champagne to passengers under twenty-one.)

If the suckers back in coach could see what was going on up in first class, there'd be a mutiny. But they couldn't, so I spent the five-hour flight reading magazines, watching the movie—Orlando Bloom looks even better while you're eating a warm chocolate-chip cookie—and imagining what my life would be like in Hollywood.

The fantasy went like this: My Aunt Laurel would meet me at the airport and a soft-focus tearjerker of a reunion would ensue. She'd instantly recognize my star potential and sign me up for the talent agency she runs. Of course, I'd have to pay my dues just like everyone else: a few casting agents would shake their heads slowly and say I just wasn't quite tall enough or busty enough or bimbonic enough for the part. But then a movie script starring a smart, sassy young woman would land on Laurel's desk and a few months later, I'd be wearing Dior at the film premiere. (The Dior would be free, of course—I read *Us Weekly*, I know what's up.) And then the film offers and interview requests would start rolling in. The people who had spent the first half of senior year making my life a living hell (Brynn Kistler and Bryan Dufort, I'm looking at *you*) would all be sorry, but it would be—that's right—*too late*. I wouldn't deign to speak to Bryan or even Jeff, my so-called best friend. Because I'd already be dating somebody who really appreciated me: Orlando Bloom.

And then we touched down at LAX and the fantasy evaporated everything started to go wrong.

First, the airline lost my luggage. This had never happened to me before; maybe it was karmic compensation for flying first class. Then, while I was standing at the baggage claim, staring at the shiny metal chute and telling myself that there was still a chance my bags could materialize at any moment, despite the fact that all my fellow passengers had collected their suitcases and left twenty minutes ago, I heard a voice behind me say, "Eva?"

I turned around to greet my aunt, resisting the urge to wipe my suddenly sweaty palms on my jeans, and came face-to-face with . . . a total stranger. A thin, blond stranger who looked about five years older than me. She had a BlackBerry in one hand, a slouchy suede purse in the other, and an impatient scowl on her Mystic Tanned puss.

Now. I may not have grown up in the big city, but I'd sat through all the obligatory school assemblies on sex, drugs, and the rising incidence of adolescent abduction. I wasn't about to go strolling off with any random, shifty-eyed man who stalked me down after swim practice. But please. If I *were* going to get kidnapped, I highly doubted my captor would be a size-two, twenty-three-year-old ice queen with a French manicure and diamond earrings the size of peanut M&M's. You just don't see a lot of perps fitting that profile on *CSI*.

So I took a few steps toward her and said, "Yeah, I'm Eva."

"Good." The blonde nodded crisply. "I'm Harper Hollings, your aunt's assistant. She sent me to pick you up. You're late."

I tried to hide my disappointment. "She didn't come to pick me up herself?"

"It's Wednesday afternoon and she has a meeting with Cameron Crowe today. She's not going to reschedule that to make an LAX run."

"Who's Cameron Crowe?"

Harper made a big show of rolling her eyes. "Hel-*lo*, he's a director and a genius and he and his producers are looking for a lead for their new movie."

"Oh."

"Yeah. And I'm covering the phones while Laurel's gone. So I don't have all day. Where's your stuff?"

I winced. "I think it's lost."

"Lost?" A dark look came over her face, the look of a Hilton sister watching someone ding her Bentley at the Neiman Marcus valet station. "You have got to be kidding me."

I could feel my dislike snowballing with every syllable out of her mouth. "Nope. I kid you not."

"What a pain in the ass." She drummed her fingers on the screen of her BlackBerry. "This is why I always fly into Burbank or Santa Monica. LAX is like that scene at the end of

*Titanic* where all the plebs are trying to get off the boat at once."

"Well, Aunt Laurel made my travel arrangements, so take it up with her," I retorted. This shut her up for a few seconds. Then she stalked over to the airline's customer service desk, stomped her feet, waved her fists, and yes, busted out the phrase, "Do you know who I work for?" (They didn't, for the record.) Once she'd wrapped up the hissy fit, she marched back to me and said, "Let's go. We're going to put this on the roof for now and follow up tonight."

"Put it on the, uh, the roof?" I glanced up at the water-stained ceiling tiles.

"Yes. It's an expression I learned right after I graduated from Harvard and moved out here to break into the business. It means we're going to leave the problem alone for now, until we have more time and information."

"Okay." Why couldn't she just say that then? And I loved how she'd managed to name-drop her Ivy League pedigree in the first ten minutes of meeting me. Retch. "But when will I get my bags? I kind of need all my stuff."

"Oh my God. What did I just say? *Yes,* you'll get your stuff *when we take it off the roof.* Hold your damn horses."

What a freak. "Fine. Whatever."

Harper led the way through the sliding glass doors and across the street to a cavernous parking garage that smelled like old fast food and car exhaust. Although she had dressed appropriately for a blizzard (white cashmere turtleneck, black wool pants, patent leather high-heel boots, and a thick black coat with a fur collar), I couldn't help but notice it was about seventy degrees outside. And sunny.

"Wow." I peeled off my sweatshirt the moment I sat down in the passenger seat of her spotless white Infiniti coupe. "Is it always this warm in January?"

She blinked. "We're in a cold snap. Aren't you freezing?"

I shrugged. "I grew up in Massachusetts."

"Well, your blood hasn't thinned out yet. Give it a year or two. I remember how cold it used to get in the winter when I was at Harvard . . ."

And on and on. During the forty-minute drive to my aunt's agency, she managed to wedge the word "Harvard" into her monologue five more times. I counted.

We hit traffic on the freeway; eight-lane gridlock like I'd never seen. Cars were lined up for miles, sunlight glinting off the hoods. But when I remarked on this, she scoffed, "This? This is nothing. It's not even rush hour yet."

Evidently, she'd been born an expert on *everything*. But I tried to suck it up and be pleasant, for my aunt's sake, until Harper went on the offensive.

"Must be nice to be Laurel's niece. Lots of girls would give up their vital organs to have a connection at the Allora Agency."

I forced a smile. "And I didn't have to donate a single kidney. Guess I lucked out."

"It's the best teen agency in L.A. Laurel will discover the next Mischa Barton or Natalie Portman or whoever and all the casting directors know it. Do you have any idea how hard it is to get your aunt to even consider a new client? How many résumés and desperate requests for meetings she gets every single day?"

"Well . . . no?"

"Of course you don't," she spat. "Because you just happened to be born with the right last name. But I'll let you in on a little secret: nepotism only gets you so far in Hollywood. Don't think you can just coast through with Laurel's connections and a pretty face because you can't!"

Whoa. Somebody had a few too many triple espressos today. "I'll keep that in mind."

"You do that. Anyway"—she took a few calming breaths and fiddled with the radio knob—"shouldn't you be in school?"

"Not really." I stared out the window at the scraggly palm trees by the exit signs. "I graduated a semester early, and I'm taking a few months off."

"You mean you dropped out."

"No, I mean I graduated," I said evenly. "As in finished. Got my diploma."

"But you're going to college in the fall?" she pressed.

I nibbled my lower lip. "No, I got in early admission at Leighton College, but I deferred."

"Why would you do that? Leighton's a really good school."

"Oh, no reason." No reason that I wanted to think about *ever again.* "I just, you know, wanted to see the world. That's the hot thing now—taking a gap year. Like the British do."

" 'Like the British do?'" A tight little smirk played on her lips. "Uh-huh. I see."

"You see what?" I demanded.

"Nothing. It's cool." Her voice dripped condescension. "College isn't for everyone. And the corporate world wouldn't be able to function without fast-food workers and telemarketers."

My jaw hit the floor. Not only was she a freak, she was a status whore. "Listen. You don't know me, but I *did* get into college. I got a full scholarship, as a matter of fact."

The smirk got even smirkier. "Whatever you say."

Should I tell her about my formidable GPA? Should I tell her what my life had been like back in Massachusetts and why I had to leave? Should I tell her who my mother was?

No. I wasn't about to tell her any of that because she didn't deserve to know and she wouldn't care. She was the West Coast version of Brynn Kistler and I didn't have to justify myself to her.

So I simply said: "I'm planning to be a star."

She stopped gloating long enough to laugh out loud.

I slouched down into the car seat. "What?"

"You're planning to be a star. Poof! Just like that. That's priceless. And *so* original. Look out, Lindsay Lohan." She dismissed me with a wave of her hand and turned up the radio. "Planning to be a star. I can't wait to tell Laurel. She'll die laughing."

"Welcome to Los Angeles, pet. You ready to be a star?" Aunt Laurel hung up her phone and engulfed me in a giant hug the minute I set foot in her office. Over her shoulder, across the polished cherry furniture and sleek chrome accessories, I smiled sweetly at Harper. She just crossed her arms and seethed.

"How was your flight? Did you get any lunch? Did you remember to take your Emer'gen-C? What about those tablets I told my housekeeper to send you? Did you get those?"

While she peppered me with questions, a tiny black poodle yipped at me from a Louis Vuitton pet carrier under the desk.

"This is Rhett, my pride and joy." She hoisted the little dog right up to my face, where he snarled and snapped at my nose. "Don't worry, he hardly ever bites hard enough to break the skin."

I hadn't seen my aunt in nearly four years and I'd forgotten how much energy she had. When she really gets going, she's like the Road Runner or Speedy Gonzales in overdrive—just a blur of dark hair and pale skin with a red slash of lipstick and a cellphone glued to her ear. "Oh, just look at you! You've grown up so gorgeous! Look at that skin. Look at that hair. And your bone structure—to die for. I'll arrange for you to do some head shots ASAP"—she said this as if it were one word instead of separate initials: *asap*—"and we'll start sending you out on auditions. You look so much like your mother when she was young and famous, it's scary. Truly scary."

At this, Harper cleared her throat. "Who's your mother?"

My aunt and I exchanged a look. "Never mind," we said in unison.

Laurel snatched up the coffee cup resting on her desk and threw back the remaining dregs of java. "So! Darling! Let's go grab a bite to eat. Where's your luggage?"

"It's on the roof," I said with a nod toward Harper "the 'Har' is for Harvard" Hollings.

"Is it?" My aunt looked like she was trying to suppress a smile. "Well, I'm sure Harper will have it off the roof and in my possession by five P.M."

"Of course," Harper bit out, glaring at me when Laurel turned away.

I'd been in California for an hour and a half and already I'd met my new archenemy. A Hilary Duff to my Lindsay Lohan.

How very L.A. of me.

Now all I needed was the fame, fortune, and free Dior.

# 2

"So," my aunt said as we sat down to lunch at Kate Mantilini, a posh see-and-be-seen eatery masquerading as a homey diner, "what shall we do with you now that you're finally out here? Do you want to do print work? Commercials? Pilot season is coming up, so you might be able to snag some TV auditions. But getting SAG membership at this stage of the game could be a problem . . . do you have any modeling or acting experience?"

"Right. Like Grandma and Grandpa would really let me do any modeling after what happened to Mom." I leaned in over my poached fillet of sole (I figured that's what people in Los Angeles ate—that and salad and tofu—and I didn't want to look like a tourist, even though I was completely tantalized by the candy bar pie offered on the menu. Plus, our waiter looked like a blond Colin Farrell and I was not physically capable of pronouncing the words "candy bar pie" in front of him.) "Listen, Aunt Laurel—"

She held up her palm. "Just call me Laurel. 'Aunt' sounds so matronly and dried-up."

"Okay . . . Laurel—"

"Much better. Now where were we?" She adjusted the lapels of her black blazer. "Oh yes, Grandma and Grandpa. How are they, anyway?"

I sighed, well aware that I had just been deliberately deflected from my original point. "Good, I guess. Tired of raising a teenager."

She nodded, suddenly engrossed in her salad.

"When the guidance counselor told us that I had enough credits to graduate early, they were more excited than I was."

"I heard. They told me they were moving to Florida."

"Already sold the house," I confirmed. To a buxom blonde, according to Jeff. "They had a condo in Cocoa Beach all picked out."

"Well, they're smart to cash out of the Massachusetts real-estate market. They've been wanting to move for years now."

"I know." I picked up my fork and prodded the fish. No doubt about it; definitely should have opted for the candy bar pie. "They were just waiting for me to finish school."

My aunt finally looked up from her lettuce and tomatoes. "Eva, I know I haven't been around much while you were growing up, but I've been—"

"Working. I know. It's okay." I put down my fork. "It's not your fault my mom didn't feel like raising me."

"Don't say that." She grabbed her BlackBerry out of her purse and started punching buttons. "I have the number for an excellent therapist and I'll be happy to—"

I choked halfway through a sip of water. "No. God, no. I'm fine. Really."

"Well, if you change your mind . . ."

"I won't. But I do have one thing to ask you."

"Shoot."

"My mom . . . she's living out here right now?"

My aunt's expression stayed carefully neutral. "That's what I hear."

"Well, do you have a phone number for her? Or an address? 'Cause I thought, as long as I'm out here, I might as well call her and see if she wants to do lunch or something."

"Oh, pet." She reached over and squeezed my hand. "I don't know how to get in touch with her right now. And even if I did, well . . . I don't think you should get your hopes up."

Hmm. My grandmother had said exactly the same thing when I'd pitched this idea to her. Perhaps they'd had a "let's save Eva from herself" intervention meeting on the sly?

"Okay." I shrugged one shoulder, keeping my tone light. "But since I'm here, it couldn't hurt just to call her, right? I mean, it'd be rude *not* to."

My aunt grimaced as if someone had slipped strychnine into her salad dressing. "Are you *sure* you don't want me to set up an appointment with that therapist?"

"I don't need a psychologist's permission to call my own mother. I don't need anybody's permission."

She heaved a huge sigh, then threw up her hands. "Okay. I'll give it to you straight. You're a legal adult now; you can take it. Eva, when's the last time you saw your mother?"

I paused. "Two—no, three years ago. She came to Massachusetts for Christmas my freshman year."

"And when's the last time she called you?"

"Uh . . ."

"Yeah. That's the thing about your mom. I love her. You love her. But she's . . . she's . . ."

I rattled off a very abbreviated list of adjectives I'd heard applied to my nearest blood relative. "Irresponsible? Chaotic? An absentee parent?"

"Yes, yes, and yes." Laurel looked me straight in the eye. "And she's never going to change."

"I know."

"It's just the way she is."

"I know."

"It's not that she doesn't love you."

"I know."

"So?"

I shrugged again. "So just give me her new cell number."

"Eva, I don't have it."

"Don't worry, I'm not expecting anything."

"I *don't have it.* Hand to God."

I eyeballed her with what my grandmother referred to as the "Someone's been reading too much Sylvia Plath" stare. An uncomfortable silence stretched out between us.

"Aren't you supposed to be at the age where you're pulling *away* from your mother?" she finally said.

"Probably, but how can I pull away from her when *she's* been pulling away from *me* since I was four?"

14    BETH KILLIAN

"Fair point."

Maybe I'd worn her down enough to get what I wanted. "You really don't have her number?"

She turned her palms out. "I really don't have it."

"Fine." I decided to believe her. For now. "Since the airline lost my luggage, all I have is my carry-on. Harper says you have to work all afternoon, so should I just take a cab to your house?"

She looked surprised. "Oh, no. I thought you knew—you're not going to be staying with me."

"I'm not?" I knew she'd just bought a plush mansion in Beverly Hills with an equally plush guesthouse tucked back by the pool. I'd assumed I'd be staying there. If she wasn't going to take me in, then where was I supposed to live? Gritty images of cardboard boxes and urine-scented "youth hostels" flashed through my mind. So this was how teenagers ended up turning tricks on Sunset Boulevard. I'd have to wear fishnet stockings and microminis and color in my boot heels with permanent marker, just like Julia Roberts in *Pretty Woman*. No way was this going to work out—I couldn't even get a real date for homecoming this fall, let alone enough street corner business to pay for food and rent . . .

But my aunt wasn't quite ready to pimp me out. "Sorry, I thought your grandmother had discussed this with you. I live at the office, for all intents and purposes. It would be completely impractical for you to move in with me—you'd be isolated and lonely all day with no way to get around unless I gave you the keys to my BMW, which is never going to happen. I love you, but I don't love anybody enough to let them drive my Beamer. So you're going to live in the agency apartment building in West Hollywood."

"I get my own apartment?" Sweet!

"Not exactly. The agency leases a small building to house some of our teenage clients."

"Really? You have a whole apartment building?"

"Don't get your hopes up; it's hardly the Ritz. But yes, we have a building. We needed a place to put all the kids who come out to L.A. for pilot season without their parents, or who are old enough to have their own place but whose parents want them to have a little supervision."

I nodded slowly. "And I'm supposed to be the supervision?"

"Not exactly. We have what I guess you might call a den mother—she's the mom of one of our girls, you'll meet her later—but I want you to help her out when you're not working with me. Be my eyes and ears, make sure no one's involved in anything too scandalous, that's all."

She picked *me* to head up the scandal patrol? Oh, the irony.

"You'll get a cellphone, a monthly stipend, and your own bedroom," she continued. "If everything works out, maybe I can even be convinced to lease you a car."

Hang on. This seemed way too good to be true. I squinted in the sunlight pouring through the plate glass windows and tried to figure out why my aunt, a woman not known for selfless sacrifice, was being so magnanimous.

My train of thought derailed as the dreamy blond waiter ("Gavin," according to his name tag) floated by. Yum. Where did guys like that come from? Not Alden, Massachusetts, that was for damn sure. I wondered how old he was. I wondered if he was straight. I wondered if he had a weakness for unusually tall, flat-chested brunettes. (What? It could happen.)

"Eva?" My aunt's tone made me suspect that this was not the first time she'd said my name.

I tried to roll my tongue back into my mouth. "Yeah?"

"Everything okay?"

"Everything's great. And the apartment sounds fantastic. But I have to ask: what's the catch?"

"No catch," she insisted, a little too quickly. "I mean, you'll have a few roommates, but . . ."

I narrowed my eyes. "How many roommates?"

"Don't you dare pull a star trip on me already. You've been out here less than twenty-four hours, so shut your yap and just be grateful I managed to get you your own bedroom." And we were back to the real Aunt Laurel.

"Thank you," I said meekly.

"You're welcome."

"So what exactly am I going to be doing with your agency? Besides making my name as an international superstar?"

Your job is to work on your acting skills, learn about the business, and help keep everyone in line. No drugs, no underage drinking, no tabloid reporters going through the trash, etc."

"So basically, I'm going to be the narc everyone hates?"

She nodded. "Think of it as *in*sensitivity training. Then, when you're famous and *Star* magazine splashes unflattering photos of you on the cover and spreads filthy rumors about your allegedly bisexual boyfriend, you'll already be toughened up and it won't bother you a bit."

I couldn't protest, though God knows I wanted to. I needed a place to live. That was the problem with not having a proper set of parents—I was always dependent on someone else's generosity. My friends in Massachusetts took my breath away with the frequency and enormity of their familial demands—new cars, eight-hundred-dollar prom dresses, permission to stay out all night with college guys. Their parents just shrugged and gave in. My situation, on the other hand, always felt precarious. I'd hoped to leave that behind when I boarded the plane for Los Angeles, but now I realized how naïve I'd been. I was now at an age where I should be able to take care of myself, except I had no idea how to begin doing that.

So I choked down another bite of sole and mumbled, "Okay, whatever you need."

"That's what I love about you: always so reasonable. And don't worry, you'll make plenty of friends." She said this like I was a pigtailed little Brownie heading off for my first summer at sleepover camp. "I put you in with Coelle Banerjee. She's a doll, an absolute living doll."

"So it'll be me and Coelle Banerjee, the living doll, in a two-bedroom apartment?"

"Actually, it's a three-bedroom unit." Suddenly my aunt was obsessed with her coffee cup, flagging down the impossibly handsome Gavin for a refill, examining her manicure.

I sighed. "Who's the other girl?"

She pretended to be confused. "The other girl? You mean the third roommate?"

"Yes, the third roommate."

"Well, we wanted to put you in with the potential trouble-maker. Because, um, you're such a good influence. So responsible."

"Uh-huh." If only she knew.

"Her name is Jacinda. Jacinda Crane-Laird. You're going to love her. She's very charming, very sophisticated."

I frowned. "Jacinda Crane-Laird? Where have I heard that name before?"

"Oh, I'm not surprised you've heard of her. She's my hottest up-and-coming client." My aunt started to sound like a used-car salesman. "Blond, gorgeous, oozing panache."

All of a sudden, I knew where I had heard the name. And this realization caused me to break down and beg for dessert. I was no longer embarrassed to say the words "candy bar pie" in front of Gavin. That's how bad it was.

Obscenely rich. Totally wild. Willing to break any law, legal or physical, for a good time. That's what I'd heard about Jacinda Crane-Laird. And guess where I'd heard all that?

"Page Six," I said. "Jacinda Crane-Laird was in Page Six, right? At some premiere party?"

She looked impressed. "Very good. But what's a high schooler in the Berkshires doing reading the *New York Post* gossip column?"

"What do you think?" I rolled my eyes. "Mom sent me a copy when her name was in it."

"Your mom made Page Six? When? What'd she do?"

I covered my eyes with my hand. "Last year, December 29. There was some party at a club called Marquee and she was dancing on the tables and flashing her panties and making a fool of herself."

"Some things never change," she muttered. "December 29, huh? How do you remember these things? Do you take a lot of ginger? Ginseng? Ginkgo biloba?"

"I remember because it was my birthday." I tried to keep the bitterness out of my voice. "She didn't send me a birthday card, but she sent the Page Six clipping. By FedEx. Overnight express."

She paused. "And you're really, truly sure you want to track her down?"

"Yep. It's my life. I'll ruin it if I want to."

"Go ahead. I give up. Torture yourself if you must. Now finish that pie and let's go. I should get back to the office. We've got a slew of breakdowns to do this afternoon."

"Breakdowns?"

"Yeah. New scripts come in, we look at the descriptions of each character and figure out which client might be right for a part."

"Like 'crazy but photogenic celebutante party girl' would be perfect for Jacinda Crane-Laird?"

"Let me give you a little advice about surviving in Los Angeles: we don't do labels, judgments, or moral condemnation." She gave me a little wink. "At least, not in public. And it's not 'partying'—it's 'networking.'"

"Gag me with a spoon. Isn't that something else they say out here?"

"Only if it's 1985. Don't be so gloom and doom, pet. You could learn a lot from Jacinda."

"Like what? Isn't she famous just for being famous?" I scoffed.

"Exactly. And with my help, she's going to parlay that into movie deals, endorsements, and her own little empire of hip."

"Is that what you want for me, too?"

"Wrong question. Is that what *you* want for you?"

I shrugged. "I don't know. I guess I was hoping I'd just find my niche, and . . ."

"This is the big time: no one ever just 'finds her niche.' You have to scratch, kick, and shove your way up. I can get you in with the best head shot guy in town, I can get your name in with the best producers, but when you show up for an audition, you'll be on your own and you better *want* it. You need goals, you need focus, and you need to thrive on rejection like it's a big box of Godiva."

But wait. My mother had succeeded in Hollywood—for a little while at least—and she was the least focused person I'd ever known.

"So how do you explain Mom?" I asked.

My aunt sat back in her chair and gave me a steely, serrated smile. "How do you think I got started in this business? I was her manager. And I was damn good. But I wanted it more than she did, so once she fell apart, I kept going and built the Allora Agency with blood, sweat, and tears."

All this talk about bloodshed and battle started to alarm me. I'd come out here to broaden my horizons and get a taste of the real world, not to be bludgeoned to death in a Rodeo Drive version of Mortal Kombat.

"Uh . . ."

"So if you don't really want to do this, if you're not utterly convinced that this is your true calling and the entertainment business is pulsing through your veins and you can't live without it, you should tell me right now." She was getting agitated, displaying all the same symptoms that my grandmother did when talking about the time I streaked my hair pink (*One* time! *Two* years ago!)—cheeks flushed, fists clenched, vein popping out in forehead. "Your grandmother told me you finished high school early because you were dying to make it in Hollywood."

"She's absolutely right," I lied. "What other reason could I possibly have for graduating in December and moving three-thousand miles away?"

She stared at me for a few moments, then seized her fork and stabbed up a bite of my pie. "All right, then. We're on the same page. Now get this freaking pie out of here before I undo all my nutritionist's hard work."

"One more question . . ."

She pointedly checked her watch. "What?"

"Jacinda Crane-Laird. She's rich, right?"

"Her grandmother has a museum named after her. Her father used to own the New York Mets. What do you think?"

I nodded. "So why is she living in the agency apartment instead of a beach house in Malibu?"

"First, she's a minor. Second, she's a hellcat."

I dropped my head into my hands and groaned.

"Try to keep her under control and fully clothed. Her parents are sick of their snooty old-money friends saying, 'I was so sorry to hear about your daughter's topless photos on the Internet.' If it happens one more time, they're probably going to be off Brooke Astor's guest list and then they'll have to leave the Upper East Side in disgrace and live in Palm Beach year-round."

"But if she's such a handful, why don't they just hire a nanny? Or a bodyguard?"

"She's seventeen—a bit old to have a nanny, don't you think? And as for the bodyguard, no mere bodyguard can protect a paparazzi-loving Park Avenue princess from herself. I told them I could handle her. And I can, thanks to you. Oh, and I almost forgot." She reached into her purse, pulled out her wallet, and extracted a credit card. Platinum.

"For me?" I snatched the card before she could change her mind.

"I've arranged for you to be an authorized user on this account. Your grandparents say you're very responsible for your age, so I'm going to trust you. All I ask is that you stay within a reasonable budget every month." She named a figure so outlandish, so astronomical, that I wanted to laugh and tell her I wouldn't be able to spend that in a *year*.

But I didn't. Instead, I crammed that card into my nondesigner (not for long!) bag and decided it was high time I discovered my inner fashionista.

# 3

Harper icily ignored me on the drive to the agency's apartment building. My luggage, unfortunately, was still "on the roof," so Aunt Laurel had ordered Harper to run to the drugstore and buy shampoo, toothpaste, etc., to tide me over. Little Miss Ivy League felt such errands were beneath her and gave me the silent treatment for the rest of the afternoon, which I thoroughly enjoyed.

She dropped me off in front of a run-down, two-story white stucco apartment building, pressed a key into my palm with a lot more force than necessary, and snapped, "You're apartment two. I'll pick you up tomorrow morning at eight. Be ready."

"Ready?" I blinked. "Ready for what?"

But she just readjusted her sunglasses, slammed the passenger door behind me, and peeled away from the curb, not even pausing for the STOP sign at the end of the block.

I'd call Aunt Laurel tonight and find out what, exactly, I should prep for. But first, into the den of divadom. I squared my shoulders, clutched my sad little plastic bag of toiletries, and prepared to come face-to-face with the Page Six Sex Kitten.

The apartment complex was actually pretty cute once I got through the rusting metal gate. A wall of mailboxes gave way to a small, open courtyard surrounded by doors labeled one through six. I slipped my key into the lock and turned the knob, holding my breath and steeling myself for whatever lurked behind door number two.

"Mom! How many times do I have to tell you? I'm not going to New York this weekend! I have an SAT prep course class on Saturday and I can't miss another one!" A willowy girl with glossy black hair, soulful brown eyes, and skin the color of café au lait was standing in the middle of the room, throwing blueberries and flax seeds into a blender and yelling in the direction of the phone. She wore baggy jeans and a Cornell University sweatshirt, but I could tell she was tiny under all those folds of material.

The red speakerphone light blinked on as a disembodied voice flooded through the room. "Coelle. We're talking about a Tampax commercial. National exposure, huge residuals. Think what it'll mean for your career! They asked for you specifically. I already spoke with Laurel about this and she agrees one hundred percent. I know this prep course is important to you, but try to keep it in perspective. You can study on the plane."

"Not for the essay section, I can't, and that's what I need help with! And how am I ever going to get into a decent pre-vet program if I can't crack six hundred fifty on the critical reading section?"

The speakerphone sighed impatiently. "If you'd just listen to me for once, you wouldn't need to worry about SAT scores. All the good colleges are looking for kids with special talents, and what could be more special than a feminine hygiene commercial? All I'm asking is—"

"For me to put my whole life on hold until I win an Oscar? That's never going to happen, Mom. Are you listening to me? Never."

"Well, not with that attitude, it's not. Do you know how many girls your age would kill to be the face of Tampax?"

*"Argh!"* The girl slammed the lid on the blender, plugged it in, and turned it on full blast for at least thirty seconds. When the angry whirr died down, her mom was still going.

". . . and you could be the first Indian actress to win the Academy Award! You could make history! With an honor like that, you could get into any college you want! Columbia! Yale! Look at Julia Stiles and Claire Danes!"

"I have to go, Mom. My new roommate just came in."

"Okay, but what about New York this weekend? I can book your tickets tonight—"

*"I'm not going!* Leave me alone!" She marched over to the phone, lifted up the receiver, and slammed it down so hard the window panes shook. Then she turned to me, looking exhausted. "Hi. I'm Coelle Banerjee. You must be Eva?"

"Yeah, but is this a bad time? Because I can just go and find my room . . ."

"What?" She seemed puzzled. "Oh no, that was just my

mother. We have that same conversation at least four times a week."

"Wow."

"Yeah, she's your classic frustrated stage mother. Trying to live out her unfulfilled dreams of stardom through me and blah, blah, blah. She's been dragging me to open-call commercial auditions since I could chew solid food."

"And now you're at the Allora Agency?"

"Unfortunately for me, I turned out talented and good-looking."

I smiled. "But you don't want to win an Oscar?"

She didn't smile back. "My mom wants it bad enough for both of us. I try to look on the bright side: in a few years, I'll be too old for ingenue parts, and I'll have earned enough money to pay my own way through school so I won't owe her anything ever again."

"How old are you?"

"Seventeen." She gave me an appraising look. "So you're the newest new girl."

"You get a lot of new girls?"

"Yeah, but most of them don't last long, especially with Jacinda."

"Why?" I asked suspiciously. "What's Jacinda's deal?"

She ignored this. "Come on, I'll show you around." She gestured to the kitchen with faux wood laminate on the cabinets and peeling gold-specked linoleum on the floor. "Here we have the downstairs. The fridge has three shelves, one for each of us." She yanked the door open and pointed out an empty wire rack. "We try to keep the living room clean—well, *I* do, anyway—but . . ." The living room was blanketed in trendy clothes and accessories, like Gwen Stefani's closet had exploded in our foyer. I could barely discern patches of beige carpet and threadbare lavender sofa under mounds of inside-out jeans, blouses, skirts, and shoes. Oh, the shoes. Stilettos, sneakers, thigh-high black boots, all jumbled together with purses and the occasional tube of lip gloss.

"Upstairs are the three tiny bedrooms and one tiny bathroom." She pointed up the staircase. "That's kind of a problem, especially given the grooming habits of a certain—"

"Voilà, here I am! Now what are your other two wishes?" A model-thin blonde with waist-length hair, bloodshot green eyes, and the palest complexion I'd ever seen burst through the apartment door. Even in high heels, she stood about five foot two and carried a bulging Kitson shopping bag in each hand. "Thank God you're here. I'm having the day from hell. I missed my audition this morning because I spent the night at Trevor's—you know, the singer from the Lockbox Monkeys?"

Coelle just looked at her.

"You are so pathetically unhip, do you know that? Just wait two months—he'll be all over the radio. Anyway, of course rock stars don't believe in alarm clocks, so I overslept. And all he wanted to do this morning was smoke weed and eat Lucky Charms. So finally, I convinced him to take me to lunch at Bastide and they threw me out for talking on my cellphone. Threw me out! Can you imagine?" She paused for a dramatic sigh. "I am so hungover I could die, literally drop dead. I'll give you two hundred dollars cash if you'll run to the store and get me some Aleve. And a huge order of french fries. The greasier, the better."

I cleared my throat. "Make it three hundred and you've got a deal."

"Done." She rummaged through her purse, tossing crumpled bills on the coffee table. "Who the hell are you?"

Coelle gave her a pointed look. "Jacinda. This is Eva Cordes."

"Our roommate du jour?" She didn't even look up from her wallet. "Pleasure to meet you. Enjoy your stay at our fabulous chateau and don't let the door hit you on the way—"

Coelle cleared her throat. "Jacinda. Open your ears. This is Eva *Cordes,* our *agency owner's* niece?"

The blond head snapped up. "Oh my God, I can't believe it. Laurel actually followed through this time. She sent you here to baby-sit me, didn't she? Keep me out of trouble? Make sure I don't stay out all night with rock stars and straggle home with a wicked hangover and a bag full of Brazilian thongs?"

How to answer this tactfully? "Not really. I'm trying to get started as an actress."

"Oh. Okay." She obviously didn't believe me. "Well, then, do me a favor and forget everything I just said. I won't give you a bit of trouble, I swear. All I need are french fries and a nap and I'll be your dream roommate forever."

"She's lying," Coelle stage-whispered.

"I never lie—lying is *très* tacky." Jacinda sashayed over to the freezer, dumped a full tray of ice cubes into a dishtowel, and applied the cold compress to her forehead. "I hope you weren't kidding with that offer to go get the Aleve and the fries. I'm about to pass out from the pain."

Coelle glanced at me. "Yeah, we'll do it," she said. "And you don't even have to pay us three hundred dollars."

"I take back everything I said about you being pathetically unhip."

"Just take me with you to your waxing appointment."

Jacinda slammed her homemade compress onto the countertop. "Oh shit, is that today?"

"The salon called this morning to remind you."

This was met with a long, anguished whimper.

"I could take your place, if you want," Coelle offered.

"No, no, I have to go," Jacinda said. "It's been almost a month since my last bikini wax. You can imagine the follicle riot down there."

"Ew. I'd rather not." Coelle wrinkled her nose. "I need to come with you, though. I have a few follicle problems of my own and I'm scheduled to film a swimsuit scene next week. Come on, you can get them to squeeze me in." Her gaze shifted over to me and she sighed wearily. "Eva, too, I guess."

"Me?" I repeated, alarmed.

"Her?" Jacinda looked outraged.

Coelle gave Jacinda a long, hard stare. "She's Laurel's niece and we're going to make her feel welcome, capeesh?"

Jacinda flipped her hair and exhaled, all put-upon. "Fine. She can come."

"Oh no, that's okay," I assured them. "I'm good right now. No wax needed."

This was a bit of—okay, a lot of—a lie: I had never gotten a bikini wax in my life for multiple reasons, including limited access to full-service spas, my lifelong aversion to unnecessary pain, and my disappointing lack of a sex life thus far (unless you counted the homecoming disaster with Bryan Dufort, which I did *not*. Are you listening, Jeff?).

Jacinda arched an eyebrow at me and said, "Don't take this the wrong way, but you really should come with us. You're in dire need of a makeover."

"Jacinda Crane-Laird. Do not start," Coelle warned.

"What? She needs a facial, a manicure, and a good cut and color. Am I lying? This is a tough business and she's never going to make it with that long, limp, blah hair."

I crossed my arms. "This is the best you can get in Alden, Massachusetts."

"Well, your stylist should be beaten like a piñata. The cut is all wrong for your face. You've got great bone structure, great skin, why hide it? You've definitely got a dusky, exotic thing happening."

"I'm part French, part Peruvian," I said. And part whatever my dad was, but we didn't really need to get into that right now.

"Cool," Coelle said. "I'm half Indian, half Italian."

Both of us looked at Jacinda, who smiled and struck a pose. "One hundred percent hottie."

I tried to keep a straight face. "It's so nice to meet an adolescent who doesn't have low self-esteem."

"Isn't it? Insecurity is so boring. Who wants to hear about how you hate your thighs or your butt or your belly pooch or whatever? It's like, either get lipo or learn to deal with it and shut up, already."

"Wow. It really *is* so simple. How do you not have your own talk show?" Coelle asked dryly.

"That's a good question. I'll pitch that idea next time I run into a hot TV producer at Dan Tana's." She turned back to me. "So what kind of bikini waxes do they do out there in Alden, Massachusetts? Brazilian? Playboy? Sphinx?"

"Um . . ." *Sphinx?* WTF kind of jacked-up perversity was *that?* "Just regular, I guess."

"Regular?" Jacinda sneered, like I'd just started to whine about my belly pooch.

"Regular?" Even Coelle looked shocked and appalled. "As in, just the basics? You don't get to pick out a little Swarovski crystal design to put over the landing strip?"

Damn. Guess I should have gone with Playboy. "Well . . ."

"Oh, come on. That doesn't even count. I'll get Damascus to give you the full Sphinx treatment," Jacinda decided. "Then Marcello will do damage control on you hair."

"You'll feel so much better," Coelle assured me. "There's nothing like a good wax to cure jet lag."

Was this some sort of sadistic Hollywood hazing ritual? "But—"

"No need to thank us." Jacinda grinned. "Just don't report me next time I have to do a little extracurricular networking at Forty Deuce."

Ouch. Ouch. Ouch, ouch, ouch.

Oh, and while we're on the subject: *ouch.*

All the rumors I'd heard about bikini waxes—the redness, the swelling, the sanity-severing pain—couldn't begin to prepare me for the actual experience. Jacinda kept yelling through the door that my apprehension was making things worse ("Stop whimpering! You have to suffer to be beautiful!"), but that was bull—the whippet-thin and deceptively sweet-looking Damascus didn't need any help from me to ratchet up the wince factor.

"You people pay good money to have your first layer of skin

ripped off?" I breathed once I'd put my jeans back on and minced gingerly over to the salon chair of the great hair wizard Marcello.

"Stop your bitching. If you're going to keep up with me, this is just the tip of the iceberg." Jacinda waved her emery board at me from her perch in the neighboring stylist's chair. While a salon assistant folded peroxide-smeared squares of aluminum foil into her bangs, she passed the time by sawing away at her nails and tossing out authoritative pronouncements. "Here—have a few ibuprofen and settle down. Marcello hates it when you bring negative chi into his studio."

"It's a salon," Coelle said.

"*Mais non.* He's an artist—therefore, it's a studio."

Salon, studio . . . either way, the famous Marcello (think the body of Nick Lachey, the face of Johnny Depp, and the sensibility of J. Lo) made short work of my hair. "I know what I'm doing," he insisted as he attacked my hair with a straight razor. "Your job is to sit up straight and look like a superstah."

Which I tried to do, even though increasingly longer locks of my thick black hair were fluttering to the floor.

"Okay, but are you sure—"

"Silence!" he barked. "Superstahs do not interrupt the stylist!"

"So true," Jacinda agreed. She'd given up on her nails and was now leafing through a local newspaper called *South of Sunset* in the chair next to me. "We know what we're doing, trust us." She frowned over at Marcello's work in progress. "Take off a few more inches."

Marcello hesitated. "You think?"

"Shorter." She nodded.

I held up a hand. "But—"

"Shorter!" she yelled. "Don't argue with the master!"

A few lowlights, a deep-conditioning rinse, and a lot of razor slashes later, my hair was about a foot shorter and I looked . . .

"Perfect," according to Marcello.

"Absolutely fantastic," cooed his assistant.

"Hmmm," was Coelle's only comment.

"But . . ." I fingered the layered fringe that now brushed my neck. "It's so . . . so . . . short."

Marcello was rapidly losing his patience. "It was too long before. Now you are a woman of the world."

"Instead of Heidi of the Swiss Alps," Jacinda added.

"But my eyes." I gulped. The new style emphasized my cheekbones, which was good, but my eyes had always been a little large for my face and this cut was making it worse. "I look like one of those Precious Moments figurines."

"Oh my God, Laurel's in the paper!" Jacinda shoved *South of Sunset* over at us, jabbing her finger at a gossip column called The G-Spot with Gigi Geltin.

"She is? What'd she do?" Coelle crowded in next to me. "It's tough to get into this column. Only the truly A-list dirt makes the cut."

We hunched in and read together:

> This just in from the déjà vu depart-
> ment: Now that Duran Duran is mak-
> ing a comeback, we should have known
> that L.A.'s friskiest eighties groupie
> wouldn't be far behind. Sources tell me
> that Marisela Cordes, the face that

launched Luminous cosmetics way back when, is back in town and still chasing those guys with guitars. Her latest beau is pinstriped financeer Tyson O'Donnell, but rumor has it that she was sharing the wealth with burned-out bassist Po Richter last Friday at Mood. Will this vampy vixen ever change her ways? Time (and Tyson!) will tell. The delectable Miss Mari, bunking with her power agent sis Laurel Cordes in Beverly Hill's ritziest zip code, is said to be positively glowing, more gorgeous than ever. Maybe those rumors about her plastic surgeon ex-boyfriend were true . . . ?

I stared at the tiny black print until the whole page blurred into a pulsing sea of gray.

"So if this woman is Laurel's sister, that makes her your aunt?" Coelle asked.

I kept staring at the swirling gray. "Not exactly."

From: OutOfEden@globecon.com <eva cordes>
To: descartesismybizatch@wordup.net <Jeff Oerte>
Subject: Smegma Boy
Jeff. Seriously. The whole thing with Bryan was a mistake.
For the last time, I'm sorry.
Don't you think I've suffered enough? I had to leave the
state.

From: descartesismybizatch@wordup.net <Jeff Oerte>
To: OutOfEden@globecon.com <eva cordes>
Subject: RE: Smegma Boy
Sorry, my ass. You're just sorry you got caught. I saw how
you salivated over him in bio lab last year. You said, and I
quote, "He could be an Abercrombie & Fitch model." Like
EVERY SINGLE FREAKING DAY.
I'm not as stupid as you think. Just ask the National
Merit Scholarship committee. Zing!

From: OutOfEden@globecon.com <eva cordes>
To: descartesismybizatch@wordup.net <Jeff Oerte>
Subject: (no subject)
Grow the hell up.
E.

From: descartesismybizatch@wordup.net <Jeff Oerte>
To: OutOfEden@globecon.com <eva cordes>
Subject: RE: (no subject)
YOU grow up.

From: OutOfEden@globecon.com <eva cordes>
To: descartesismybizatch@wordup.net <Jeff Oerte>
Subject: RE: RE: (no subject)
No, YOU grow up.
P.S. Have fun in AP calculus while I'm waving to my fans
on the red carpet, suckah.

From: descartesismybizatch@wordup.net <Jeff Oerte>
To: OutOfEden@globecon.com <eva cordes>
Subject: RE: RE: RE: (no subject)
No, YOU . . . wait, I can't have this argument anymore. I
have a hot date with the hot girl. (And yes, she does have
a name. Liliana. You know what that is? HOTTT.)

From: OutOfEden@globecon.com <eva cordes>
To: descartesismybizatch@wordup.net <Jeff Oerte>
Subject: RE: RE: RE: RE: (no subject)
I can't believe I ever used to like you.

From: descartesismybizatch@wordup.net <Jeff Oerte>
To: OutOfEden@globecon.com <eva cordes>
Subject: RE: RE: RE: RE: (no subject)
**I** can't believe you like Smegma Boy enough to do
what you did in his basement.

# 4

"I need to talk to Laurel right now," I yelled into Coelle's cellphone as Jacinda careened through rush-hour traffic in her silver Mercedes. (I had never been in a Benz convertible before, but given that I was crammed into the "back" of what was really a two-seater while trying to get answers about my gossip-column-fodder mother from the aunt who claimed she couldn't offer me her guesthouse because she *didn't want me to be lonely,* I couldn't say I was really enjoying the ride. Especially since Jacinda was blasting twangy country music—an odd choice for a high-society debutante who had been raised on Mozart and Chopin, but there you have it—through the state-of-the art stereo system at ear-splitting decibels.)

"Yes, you mentioned that the last time you called, twenty minutes ago." Harper stifled a yawn on the other end of the line. "But she's still out of the office."

"When will she be back?" I demanded.

"She'll be back when she gets back. You're not the most important thing in her life, you know."

"Believe me, I'm aware of that." I cringed and covered my eyes as Jacinda vroomed into the left lane, missing a U-Haul by centimeters.

"She's a major Hollywood player," Harper went on. "Just because she's doing you a favor by taking you in—"

"Yes, okay, I'm the L.A. version of Oliver Twist. Olivia Twistina, I get it. Can I at least leave a message?"

"You can do whatever you want." She paused. "This wouldn't happen to be in reference to a certain G-Spot item in today's *SOS*, would it?"

"You read that?"

"Everyone in this town reads it," she sniped. "Pet."

"I have to go."

"No message?" All saccharine concern.

"No message."

"Okay, then. By the way, you're taking head shots with Nasih Abicair on Friday and you're supposed to go to acting and movement class with Coelle and Bissy tomorrow morning at eight. I have to shuttle you around if you can't get a ride, so I strongly urge you to find one."

"Acting and movement class with Coelle and Bissy," I repeated. Coelle turned around from the front seat of the car and made a face.

"Eight A.M. sharp." Another totally fake-o yawn. "Now if there's nothing else I can do for you . . ."

"No." Which prompted a race to see who could hang up on the other faster.

"You got sucked into our A and M class?" Coelle said when I handed back her phone. "Welcome to purgatory."

"Why? What's so bad about . . ." I tried to sound all blasé and in the know . . . "A and M class?"

Jacinda started to laugh. "Nothing—if you enjoy spending your morning doing trash can mime. Or getting in touch with your inner penguin."

"And some of us *did* mind, which is why some of us got thrown out." Coelle shot her a look.

"Yeah, and look where being a good little girl gets you: stuck in class twice a week with Bissy."

"Who's Bissy?" I asked.

"You'll see." Jacinda cackled, veering across two lanes of traffic to make a last-second right turn. "You'll see."

"Hey, y'all. I've been waiting for your cute little heinies to get back!" A tanned, perky blonde met us at the front gate the moment we returned to the agency apartment building. She looked about my age and was dressed entirely in white—white sweater, white skirt, white tights, white boots—and trailed by a woman clad in magenta who was dripping in gold jewelry and had the longest manicured nails I'd ever seen in my life. "Where've all y'all been? I've been dying to meet Laurel's niece!"

"That's me." I stepped forward and offered a handshake. "I'm Eva Cordes."

"Oh, you're just breathtaking! Isn't she breathtaking, Momma?"

"Run for your life," I heard Coelle mutter behind me.

Magenta Woman smiled, which must have required considerable effort, given the tautness with which her skin was pulled across her forehead and cheeks, and looked me up and down. "Mm-hmm. You're just a precious little dollface, aren't you?"

Many, many words had been used to describe me over the course of my life, but "precious little dollface" was a new one. "Uh . . ."

"Your aunt told us all about you," Magenta Woman went on. "I'm Mrs. Darla Billington, and I'm what you might call the resident mom of the agency apartments."

"Laurel mentioned we had some kind of 'den mother,'" I said.

"Well, that's me, sugar plum. We're just one big happy family, aren't we, girls?"

Jacinda and Coelle succumbed to sudden coughing fits, all the while edging toward the door to our apartment.

Mrs. Billington grabbed the girl in white and shoved her into my personal space. "This is my daughter, Bissy."

Bissy planted her hands on her hips, stuck her right foot out in front of the left, and beamed like she was about to start turning letters on *Wheel of Fortune*.

"Pleased to meet you." I paused, trying to figure out how to say her name in a way that didn't sound like I was making fun of her. "Bissy."

"Charmed, I'm sure." She dipped down into an elegant curtsy.

"Are you an actress?" I asked. Perhaps she was starring in a remake of *Gone With the Wind* and trying to stay in character.

Bissy opened her mouth but before she could get a word out, Mrs. Billington interjected with, "Yes. She's going to be the new 'It' girl any minute now. She's got everything it takes— beauty, talent, charisma . . . she's just one or two auditions away, I can feel it."

I heard a door slam behind me—Jacinda and Coelle had left me to fend for myself.

"I was the Miss Sweet Sixteen for the great state of Texas last year," Bissy informed me. "I made it all the way to the Miss Sweet Sixteen USA pageant and I was first runner-up."

"Only because that skanky Miss Iowa flashed the judges quote-unquote 'by accident' during the swimsuit competition," her mother fumed. "But we don't need to resort to such lewd displays of flesh to make it to the top. Is that brazen little thong-wearing Iowan minx going to get a three-picture deal with Paramount? *I don't think so!*"

Yikes. Slowly, slooowly, I eased toward the path of retreat my new roommates had taken.

"White is my signature color," Bissy informed me. "And I can sing better than Mariah Carey. You want to hear?" She took a deep breath and prepared to unleash her full vocal capacity.

"There's plenty of time for that later, dumpling." Her mother laid a hand on her arm. "So, Eva. Laurel told me you graduated early." She fluffed up her Himalayan mound of bangs. "You must be a very smart girl."

"That depends on who you talk to," I hedged.

"Well, my little Bissy is practically a genius. If she weren't destined for stardom, she coulda gone to any college she wanted. Princeton practically begged her. It was pathetic, really."

Unless Princeton had innovated some Monochromatic Accesorizing degree program, I highly doubted this, but I just said, "Well, I guess you and Coelle have a lot to talk about."

"Coelle?" Mrs. Billington scoffed. "That gal's practically illiterate compared to my baby. She thinks she's such hot stuff 'cause she's applying to Cornell? Darlin', I wouldn't wipe my boots on Cornell after walking across ten miles of cowpies in the rain."

"Do you have a boyfriend?" Bissy piped up.

"No," I admitted.

"Did you leave one behind in Massachusetts?"

I stared at the ground. "Not exactly."

She leaned in, drawn to the promise of gossip like a lion to a gimpy gazelle. " 'Not exactly'? What does that mean?"

"It means . . ." It meant I left two guys behind, one I'd wanted and the other who'd wanted me, but no boyfriend, per se. "It means mistakes were made."

"Well, I have a new boyfriend," she announced importantly. "He's an actor, too—"

"Crumbcake, that is *enough*." Mrs. Billington glared at both of us. "Don't talk her ear off; she just got here."

"But Momma, I was only—"

"You keep flaunting that boy of yours and you're going to lose him. How many times do I have to tell you?"

Bissy whipped around and hissed, "Oh, I am not, I'm ten times prettier than her and I dress better besides."

*Meow.*

Her mother gasped and whispered, "A pageant queen does not talk that way!" while I frowned down at the comfy jeans (that—yes! Okay! Could stand a quick trip to the Laundromat! But still!) I'd thought would get me through another few months.

Mrs. Billington turned to me with a bright, totally insincere smile. "Ooh, I know y'all are going to be best friends."

"We sure are!" Bissy looked ready to whip out a baton and lead a band down the football field. "Are you coming to acting and movement class tomorrow morning?"

I nodded.

"You'll ride with us." This was a command, not a request.

"Well, actually, Coelle . . ."

"Are we still jawin' about that little wannabe?" Mrs. Billington rolled her heavily mascaraed eyes. "Fine, she can come, too, but y'all better be on time. We are on our way to the *top* and we don't have time for slackers. Right, Bissy?"

When I finally escaped back to the apartment, Jacinda and Coelle were sprawled out on the sofas, flipping through magazines.

"Somebody could've warned me, *y'all,*" I grumbled. "Thanks a lot for fleeing the scene."

They looked at each other and grinned.

"You're not really an Allora girl until you've survived a Darla Billington interrogation," Coelle said.

"She does that to all the new arrivals?"

"Just the girls," Jacinda corrected. "The boys get the sugar and spice and everything nice routine. So she can harvest them for little Miss Sweet Sixteen."

"Where *are* the boys, anyway?" I asked. If they looked anything like Gavin the waiter, I might have to do a little harvesting myself.

"They're in a separate building over on Waring." Coelle didn't look up from *Cosmo*. "Don't get your hopes up, though. Most of them are gay, already taken, or bigger drama queens than Jacinda."

"Please. I could never live up to the standards they set."

A long, awkward pause ensued. Finally, my stomach rumbled and I ventured, "Does anyone feel like getting some dinner?"

Coelle shook her head. "I have to go running before it gets too dark." She nodded at Jacinda. "You coming?"

"Hell no, I'm hungover." Jacinda made a face. "And I don't do cardio. It's so nineties."

Coelle didn't ask if I wanted to go. Which was just as well; after all the traveling and bikini waxing and gossip column reading about my mother, the last thing I wanted to do was run five miles. But it would've been nice to be asked.

"Well, then . . . I better go unpack."

Neither of them looked up as I grabbed my plastic bag of toiletries and headed up the stairs, but once I was out of sight, I heard Coelle say, "Well, she lasted six hours so far; that's longer than the last roommate."

"You say that as if I were somehow responsible." Jacinda giggled.

The only open door upstairs led to a small, empty bedroom. My new sanctuary: four blank white walls with a low ceiling, frayed beige carpet, and the smell of fresh paint fumes. I opened the window and curled up on the twin mattress (no sheets) against the wall.

Finally, I could stop wondering if I was way out of my league in Los Angeles.

Because now I *knew* I was.

# 5

I slept in my clothes that night, huddled under the soft chenille throw I borrowed from the living room couch, and woke up in a spectacularly bad mood. I was groggy, I was PMSing, and my AWOL mother was holed up in my treacherous aunt's Bev Hills guesthouse, still making the gossip pages and acting like she was my age. Well, acting like I *would* act at my age had I been born with normal parents to a normal childhood.

As I lurched out of my room toward the stairs, the door across the hall popped open and Coelle stuck her sleepy face out.

"Oh good, you're up."

"Yeah, I have to call my grandparents. Can I use the phone downstairs?"

She frowned. "Don't you have a cellphone?"

I didn't have a cell because my grandparents were irrevocably convinced that they gave teenagers: a) brain cancer, and b) too much freedom. I'd bought one on the sly last summer, but my grandmother had confiscated it during one of her routine searches of my private property. I know. It's called "boundaries," people. But they seemed to feel that it was *actually* called "don't turn out like your mother," so I was languishing in technological solitary confinement again.

I sensed this story would earn nothing but scorn from Coelle, so I just said, "I don't have a calling plan for California yet."

"Okay, but don't call long distance all the time because Laurel will go off on one of her 'I'm not running a charity' rants. And hurry up—we have to get to A and M class." She squinted at my rumpled outfit.

"The airline lost my luggage," I explained.

"Are you always this needy?" She rolled her eyes. "Fine. I'll lend you some sweats."

A faint electronic glow emanated from her room, so I asked, "Are you playing video games in there?"

"I'm writing a paper on *Hamlet*. It's due today and I still need two more pages."

"You guys go to school?" I don't know why I was so surprised. I mean, they were teen stars, not juvvies.

"I have a tutor on-set. Four hours a day. And Jacinda—"

"Is still sleeping, so take the conversation downstairs!" A muffled yell came from the doorway next to Coelle's.

"We'll talk in the car," Coelle muttered. "Meet you downstairs in fifteen minutes."

Twenty minutes later, hair combed, teeth brushed, and decked out in Coelle's Cornell University College of Veterinary Sciences T-shirt and black yoga pants, I clambered into Mrs. Billington's Volvo station wagon along with Coelle and Bissy who, true to form, wore a pristine white track suit and a white ribbon tied around her ponytail.

A quick call to my grandparents had yielded no new juicy information about what my mom was doing in Aunt Laurel's guesthouse. They claimed to know nothing about it, to have misplaced her phone number (Lies! Lies!), and said I should stop obsessing about Mom and focus on being Laurel's loyal little toady. (They were horrified when I told them that Laurel had entrusted me with an actual charge card. So horrified that I decided not to divulge that I had already blown through over half my monthly allowance at the salon yesterday. Oops. I'd just cut back on frivolous expenses for the next few weeks. Easy, right?)

Then I called my aunt's office number and left a voice mail announcing that the jig was up and I wanted to have brunch with her *and* my mom this weekend.

"So what is this set you're on with the tutor?" I asked Coelle as Mrs. Billington slipped a Barry Manilow CD into the car's stereo system. "Yesterday, you said you had to do a swimsuit scene?"

"Oh . . . you know," she said vaguely, suddenly transfixed by the scenery outside. "Just this show I'm on."

"She's got a recurring role on *Twilight's Tempest,*" Bissy announced from the front seat. "She plays Hester Higgenbotham, beautiful but troubled heiress to the Higgenbotham fortune, and right now she's being stalked by these deranged Chinese mafia hit men because it turns out she was switched at birth with the *real* Hester Higgenbotham, only her mom—her adoptive mom, not her birth mom—doesn't want the real Hester to be found because she has this secret past—"

"Let's just say it's nothing I'll be putting in my Cornell application and leave it at that," Coelle said sharply.

I leaned in, hungry for more details. "I've never met anyone who's actually on TV."

"Well, now you have," Bissy informed me. "We've all been on TV—Coelle, Jacinda, practically all Laurel's clients. Including me, of course. But I don't audition for TV spots anymore. Only film."

"That's right, my little orange blossom," Mrs. Billington cooed. "You're too good for some trashy soap opera. And the pay's not even that good."

Coelle pulled an iPod out of her purse and jammed the headphones into her ears.

I blinked. "Ouch."

"The truth hurts, but if you're going to make it in Hollywood you have to deal with reality." Bissy beamed beatifically. "Either you've got what it takes or you don't. That's not mean, that's a fact of life, right, Momma?"

"Move from your chin!" a purple-haired man with a black tank top and colorful tattoos adorning both arms screamed as Coelle and I walked through the door of the dance studio. "Your *chin!*"

"What's he talking about?" I whispered.

"It's a getting-into-character thing," she replied. "You'll see."

"Stay limber! Stay loose! Stop thinking; I can *see* you thinking!" he yelled at a frail-looking redhead who was flapping her arms while spinning on tiptoe. "Acting is about stripping down to raw emotion! Unleash your primal beast!"

Coelle consulted her watch. "One minute down, fifty-nine to go. Come on, I'll introduce you." She dragged me across the polished hardwood floor.

"Smith, this is Eva." Coelle shoved me in front of him like a human shield. "Laurel's niece? I think the agency called about her?"

"Ah, yes." Smith stopped haranguing the redhead and assessed me with intense, pale blue eyes. "The niece. And what is it that you do, exactly?"

I tried to take a step back, but Coelle wasn't budging.

"Well, I . . . what do you mean?"

"Do you dance, model, act?"

I tried to conjure up a Bissy Billington-esque smile. "I, um, I'm still finding my niche."

He looked like he'd just sucked on a lemon.

"I took ballet lessons for four years," I hastened to add. "When I was three."

"Why?" Smith threw up his hands. "Why does Laurel insist on sending the lost causes to me? Does she hate me? Is she trying to start a blood feud?"

I stomped on Coelle's toes, forcing her to give me some room.

"All right, all right, let's see you walk," he commanded, clapping his hands so that everyone in the room stopped talking and stared at us.

Maybe I hadn't heard him correctly. "Walk?"

"Yes." He pointed across the floor; instantly everyone skittered to the side. "Walk. To that corner and back."

I felt the blood draining out of my head. "But . . ."

"And *wow* me. I want my heart to friggin' *stop*, got that?"

I couldn't see anything but little white dots. "But . . ."

"Move!" he bellowed so loudly the redhead let out a squeak of alarm.

Okay, this was how I walked: imagine Gisele Bundchen strutting down the catwalk, hips jutted, chin tilted, working her five-inch stilettos like she was born in them . . . and then imagine the *total opposite of that*. After a startled hop, I power walked to the corner and back, head down, arms crossed defensively over my chest, trying to hide my face behind my hair (which, thanks to Marcello's pricey hatchet job, I could no longer do).

Then I tucked myself behind Coelle and prayed for spontaneous combustion. A deathly hush enveloped the room.

"What was that?" Smith demanded.

I hunched down farther behind Coelle.

"You are aging me before my time. Do you hear me? Aging me! Before my time!"

Obviously, if "walking" had been an AP course at my school, I would not have graduated early. Or at all. Ever.

"You tell your aunt I'm charging you double," Smith announced, then turned his tat-riddled back on me. "Now grab a mat and warm up, people. Obviously, you don't have any time to waste."

Coelle offered me a mint as she headed off to grab a yoga

mat from the stack by the door. A gesture of empathy? Or merely a sign that my breath reeked? Who could tell?

"Don't listen to that no-neck punk, yo," came a voice to my left. "You got super mad walking skillz fo' real."

I whirled around. "What?"

A short, skinny boy with bleached white hair and a gigantic Raiders jersey nodded approvingly. "I'd follow you and your walk anywhere, shorty."

Why? Why me? Had Jacinda crept into my bedroom last night and written "If you've been smoking old crack, come hit on me" on my forehead?

"Um . . . okay. Whatever." I started back toward the yoga mats.

But he would not be ignored. "I'm C Money Marx. Future West Side rap phenom, keepin' it real, and y'all better recognize." He grinned, revealing—no lie—an actual gold-capped tooth.

I avoided eye contact and kept moving.

He continued to leer at me, jingling the diamond-encrusted chains around his neck (which, as Bissy later pointed out, were "not part of the approved acting and movement class ensemble").

For the next fifty-five minutes, Smith barked orders at us like, "Now your character is earthy. Show me earthy! No, you're acting with your mind, not your body! Give me earthy or give me death!" and "If you're going to be a model, you have to learn to lead with your groin."

And every two minutes, the new millennium's answer to Vanilla Ice was back in my face, nodding approvingly and making lewd comments about leading with my groin.

By the end of class, I was teary with humiliation and pain—my poor defenseless hip sockets had practically been dislocated thanks to all that groin-leading—when C Money sidled up and asked me out.

Well, at least, I *think* he was asking me out. It was a little hard to decipher, but he wanted to know if I was down for a ride in his sweet new Hummer H2 ("it's macfreezy with the A-1 special sauce") seeing as I was "da love sponge."

This little love sponge said hells no.


"Evie, pet, I know you're upset, but you have to believe I was trying to look out for your best interests," were Aunt Laurel's first words when she finally called me back at the apartment that afternoon.

"Don't give me that! You lied!" I raged. "You said you didn't know where Mom was or how to reach her."

"I was trying to protect you."

"No, you were trying to make life easier for yourself." I stalked back and forth across the living room, kicking a path through Jacinda's discarded designer clothes. "I trusted you! I thought you were the one person in this family who would be honest!"

"I am, but you have to realize—"

"Then what was all that crap about, 'You're an adult now and I'll give it to you straight'?"

"You had just gotten into town. I didn't want to frontload you with drama and disappointment."

"She's my mother!" I yelled. "I have a right to call her! I have a right to see her! If there's going to be drama and disappointment, I have a right to that, too!"

"You say that, but you don't mean it," Laurel sniffed.

I ground my heel into a Narciso Rodriguez silk skirt, ripping the seam. *"Yes, I do!"* I took a deep breath and tried to lower my voice before the neighbors called the police. "She's *my* mother. I can handle her."

"Damn that Gigi Geltin," she muttered. I could hear Rhett the poodle yipping in the background. "Try to calm down and be professional about this."

"Professional about what? The fact that my mother doesn't give a rat's ass or the fact that the rest of you think you can make me feel better by lying to my face?"

"Evie." Her patience was wearing thin. "Have dinner with me tonight. We'll talk about this like rational adults."

"Can't," I said loftily. "I'm busy. Recovering from the trauma of A and M class."

"Yes, Smith left me a message this morning. Something about a blood feud?"

"He's a sadist," I informed her. "Probably kicks puppies for fun."

"He's a bit of a prima donna, yes, but he's the very best at what he does. Now stop sulking and let's pick a time for dinner. I have a few things I need to discuss with you." Her voice took on a militant, no-nonsense quality. "Do you like Italian? Ago is within walking distance from your apartment."

"I'm only going if you have my luggage," I snitted. Lies or no lies, I needed my stuff. Coelle had started to make pointed remarks about how she wasn't a one-woman Goodwill; plus the all-Cornell, all-the-time ensemble was getting old.

"I'm not going to bribe you," she said, and then in the next breath, "But as a matter of fact, Harper did get your luggage off the proverbial roof. I'll bring it with me to the restaurant. Ago. Seven. Be there."

"Ago. Seven. Got it." When I hung up the phone, Jacinda finally emerged from her bedroom, barefoot and pulling her tousled blond hair back into a ponytail.

"You're going to Ago?" She rubbed at her eye with the back of her hand. "When? Tonight?"

"Maybe," I said warily. "Who wants to know?"

"The fashion police, that's who." She sneered at my borrowed clothes. "I hope you're not wearing that."

I shrugged one shoulder. "It's this or nothing."

"Go with nothing," she advised.

"Thanks for your help." I tried to push past her, but she refused to budge in the narrow hallway.

"Why so defensive?" She grinned. "You only have, like, petticoats and sweater vests?"

"No," I replied, stung. "The airline lost my suitcases and I'm not getting them back until tonight."

"You really are helpless, aren't you?" She sighed, the original martyr in Missoni. "Come on, grab your purse. We're going to the Beverly Center. Someone has to educate you in the fine art of SoCal fashion."

I tilted my head. "Why are you being nice to me all of a sudden?"

"Keep asking questions like that and I'll change my mind," she warned. "Grab your purse. I don't have all day."

I grabbed my purse. "Fine. Thank you. But P.S., just so you know, I wouldn't be caught dead in a sweater vest."

• • •

I tried not to think about the burgeoning balance on my aunt's credit card—Laurel owed me some serious retail therapy after what she'd pulled with my mom.

Jacinda marched me from Bebe to Bloomingdale's to Betsey Johnson, leaving dressing rooms full of discarded dresses and halter tops in our wake. Skirts, sweaters, blazers, boots . . . I let Jacinda talk me into a whole new wardrobe. She even found me some great bargains on the clearance racks.

Maybe she wasn't so diabolical, after all.

When the sales clerks rang up my purchases and I was confronted with the staggering price of looking good in L.A., I just smiled and handed over my plastic. "Charge it."

From: OutOfEden@globecon.com <eva cordes>

To: descartesismybizatch@wordup.net <Jeff Oerte>

Subject: my glamtastic new life

Spent the last 2 days at the mall and the salon with my new roommates (who are SO great; we're like sisters already) getting a Hollywood makeover.

I hate to brag, but I am so gorgeous now, I make Brynn Kistler look like Steve Buscemi.

Someday, you'll be able to say you knew me before I got $25 million a picture. Lucky you.

I see you guys have a blizzard headed your way. Too bad. I'll think of you when I'm working on my tan at the beach.

Ciao,

E.

"Holy shit," Aunt Laurel said, the instant she saw me at the hostess stand at Ago. "What *happened* to your hair?"

This derailed me from my intended goal of starting round two about all her lying and deception. "You don't like it?"

"No," she said bluntly. "It looks like ass. You had such gorgeous, glossy, perfect hair. Why wasn't I consulted about this?"

I paused.

"Well? I'm waiting. Who told you to go *G.I. Jane*?"

Damn that Jacinda. "No one. I just thought I needed a makeover."

"Well, you thought wrong." She crossed her arms. "You

know who looks good with hair that short? Halle Berry and Cameron Diaz. *Not you.*"

"Sorry," I muttered. "But eventually it'll grow—"

"What am I going to do with you now?" she demanded. "You'll have to get extensions before Friday so you don't look like Sinead O'Connor in your head shots. Extensions are expensive—they're coming out of your monthly budget—"

If only she knew!

"—and they're very painful to put in, which is just what you deserve for cutting off your main selling point without running it by me."

More S&M beauty treatments. Perfect. I smoothed my new lemon yellow mohair sweater over the perilously low waistband of my new jeans as the hostess prepared to show us to our table.

Laurel stopped seething about my hair for a second. "And what the hell are you wearing?"

"Jeans?" I said hopefully. "A sweater?"

"Honey, even Britney stopped wearing jeans that low five years ago. Unless you're planning on dancing at the Seventh Veil on weekends, cover up. And that sweater—you look tubercular."

"But I was told I look good in yellow . . ."

"By whom? A colorblind saleswoman desperate for commission?"

*Damn* that Jacinda.

"Evie, if looking frumpy was a felony, you'd be on death row right now." When the hostess prepared to seat us in a busy section near the kitchen doors, Laurel snapped, "I don't think so. Do you have something a little more private?" Which got her an obsequious round of apologies and a table in the back corner.

"Much better." Her gold watch gleamed in the candlelight as she sat down and unfolded her napkin. "Never accept a first offer, pet, there's a business lesson for you."

I nodded dutifully.

"So. Are you deliberately trying to make yourself ugly?"

"No."

"Well, this has got to stop. Why don't you ask Jacinda for a few tips? She's up on all the hot new trends."

"I'll do that," I bit out.

"Good. Now let's talk about something else; I'm exhausted." She rubbed her temples as she pored over the menu. "I spent half the day screaming at a studio exec who's trying to screw one of my clients out of her back-end payouts and the other half screaming at a certain gossip columnist whose name shall not defile our meal."

I cleared my throat. "Did you talk to my mom about me yet?"

Her eyes remained firmly fixed on her menu. "Didn't get a chance. So are you settling into the apartment? What did you do today besides butcher your natural beauty?"

"Well, as you've already heard, I went to acting and movement class this morning."

The corners of her mouth tugged up. "You made quite an impression."

"Smith hates me."

"Smith hates everyone—he's a failed performance artist. Don't take it personally."

"I don't think I'm going back to class."

"Of course you are."

"I can't." I closed my eyes, trying to blot out the memory of my twenty-yard dash in front of the entire class. "It was beyond mortifying."

"That's not what I heard." She closed the menu and finally returned her full focus to me. *"I* heard you made quite a stir."

"If by 'made quite a stir' you mean 'made a complete idiot of myself,' then yes, yes I did."

"Let me finish. You met a certain young man today, yes? Caleb Marx?"

"Caleb? Oh, you mean 'C Money'? Yeah. Talk about too many freaks, not enough circuses."

"Well, he's quite taken with you."

The woman had spies everywhere. "How do you know that?"

"I heard he asked you out." Her lips thinned to a stern white line. "I also heard that you said no."

"Of course I said no. The boy is delusional. He thinks he's living in an episode of *Yo! MTV Raps* from 1995."

"Are you aware that the delusional boy's mother is Nina Marx?" She sat back, waiting for me to be impressed.

I looked at her blankly.

She exhaled loudly. "Nina Marx? The woman who can make or break an actress's entire career? The bouncer of the big time?"

My head started to hurt. "Okay, you have to remember that I just moved here yesterday from the Berkshires."

"Fine. All you need to know is that Nina is a good friend of mine and she's VP of casting for one of the major networks. She's a valuable ally, and I intend to keep her happy."

I didn't like the turn this conversation was taking. "Meaning . . . ?"

"Meaning you don't turn down her son."

"But I kind of already did."

"Then you call him and tell him you've come to your senses and you'd love to go out with him." She whipped out her BlackBerry. "I'm going to give you his number right now."

"Aunt Laurel . . ." I started.

She frowned ever so slightly.

"Laurel. Just Laurel. Sorry."

The frown vanished.

"I get that it's awkward for you, working with his mom and all, but I seriously cannot go out with him."

"You can and you will." She scribbled down a phone number and handed it to me.

"But he's so Bel Air faux ghetto. I mean, what's up with the albino hair and the gold tooth? And the perverted leering?" I shuddered at the memory. "He probably has boxes full of restraining orders and night-vision goggles stuffed under his bed."

"So he's a little rough around the edges." She shrugged. "So what? He's loaded, he's connected, and he's taken a fancy to you. All I'm asking is that you have dinner with him. Once. As a special favor to your darling, doting auntie."

I leveled my gaze and stared her down. "Why should I do you any favors after what you did to me?"

"Evie. Pet." She planted both hands on the table and leaned over toward me. "I don't ask for much from you, do I?"

"Uh . . ."

"No. I do not. But I'm asking for this. Be a trouper and go out with Nina's son. He's in a bit of a delinquent-rap-star-gangsta phase right now, but I've known Caleb since he got his first Eminem CD and he's a good kid underneath all those gold chains and basketball jerseys. I'll even let you borrow one of my Balenciaga bags and some jewelry—the good stuff—to cheer you up."

I pushed my chair back and folded my arms. "I don't want your jewelry. I want to see my mom."

She shook her head. "Eva . . ."

"Brunch. This weekend," I persisted. "Take it or leave it."

"Don't do this to me."

I held my ground. "It's a fair trade: I go out with the crown prince of poseurs, and you get my mom to come to brunch."

"I can hold your luggage hostage indefinitely, you know," she threatened.

"Mom. Saturday. Brunch. Yes or no?"

"You are *so* stubborn," she huffed. "You must take after me."

I just stared at her.

"Fine, you little extortionist, I'll see what I can do."

I smiled. "It's not extortion, it's good business."

"And under any other circumstances, I would be bursting with pride." She drummed her fingers on the pristine linen tablecloth. "Listen, I'll do my best to make this brunch happen. But I can't make any promises; you know your mother."

"Not really," I said quietly.

"This isn't going to end well."

"Why? Don't you think she'll want to see me?" I tried to keep my expression neutral.

"Of course she wants to see you. This has nothing to do with you; that's the problem. It's never about you, it's always her, her, her."

"I know. But I'm not a kid anymore. I've grown up; I'm not

so needy and exhausting, and she doesn't have to be a parent to me. We can just be . . ." I shrugged " . . . friends."

She flinched. "Oh boy."

"What?"

"You know your mom had a little problem with, uh, certain stimulants in the eighties, right?"

"You mean she was addicted to cocaine."

" 'Addicted' is a strong word," Laurel murmured, making a point of lowering her voice so nearby diners wouldn't overhear. "But yes, I will grant you that she had a few problems. And she doesn't touch the stuff anymore, but she's just replaced it with other toxic behaviors. Sabotaging herself. Dating losers. Shopping unto financial ruin."

Like mother, like daughter. "So you're saying not to expect anything from her? I know that already."

"She just isn't emotionally equipped to be the kind of mother you're hoping for."

"I'm not hoping for anything," I said breezily, taking a moment to focus on my own menu. "We're going to have brunch and catch up, that's it."

I finally looked back up at my aunt. "What?"

She shook her head. "Nothing. Let's just move on. I scheduled your head shots for Friday morning with Nasih Abicair. And I'll have Harper squeeze you in with my hairdresser for emergency damage control tomorrow."

"Thank you."

"Are you excited?"

"Yeah." I brightened. "I don't have a lot of experience in front of a camera, except for yearbook pictures, but it'll be fun, right?"

"Right." She nodded emphatically. "Nasih is an incredible photographer. And, listen, if he says anything about your nose? Just ignore it."

"My nose?" My hand instantly flew to my face. "What would he say about my nose?"

"Nothing, nothing. But just in case . . ."

"Seriously. What's wrong with my nose?" I demanded.

"Nothing."

"Then why . . . ?"

"Look, the man's a genius. What Jimmy Choo is to shoes, Nasih Abicair is to head shots. But geniuses often have rather . . . eccentric personalities. You'll be fine. But bring some Kleenex and waterproof mascara, just in case."

# 7

Laurel's credit card got another workout the next morning. I *had* to—I needed sheets and blankets and pillows. Then I went ahead and ordered some cute tops, dresses (no yellow), and jeans (with a waistband I could wear *without* a fresh bikini wax) from Bluefly.com. Hey, as long as I was going to blow my budget, I might as well go big.

"What's your glitch?" Jacinda asked, flopping down on the couch next to me. She was still clad in the lacy black camisole and panty set she'd slept in, her pasty white midriff exposed and her long platinum hair twisted into a sloppy topknot. The world's sluttiest ballerina. "You look like you just swallowed a slingback."

I gave her an ozone-piercing glare. "I know what you did."

"What?" She turned on the TV and flipped through the channels until we reached the opening credits for the sudsy drama Coelle worked on, *Twilight's Tempest.* "I didn't do anything."

"The haircut? The clothes from five seasons ago that make me look jaundiced?"

She fluttered her eyelashes. "I have no idea what you're talking about."

"It won't work," I said crisply. "You'll never get rid of me. I'm here to stay."

Her grin was positively wicked. "That's what they all say in the beginning."

She sounded so smug and casually cruel, I wanted to slap her. But instead, I matched her tone of bored self-assurance and said, "You think you're so superior because you have Daddy's trust fund and a few mentions in Page Six? Please. I've gone ten rounds with the heavyweight champion bitch of the world; I can handle you no problem. You're barely a flyweight."

Amazingly, she looked insulted. "Excuse me? I *invented* bitchy."

I mimicked her nasal, upper-crust accent. *"Au contraire, mon aimée."*

"Really." She stopped focusing on the television and turned her gleaming green eyes toward me. "And just who, may I ask, is this paragon of bitchiness?"

"Brynn Kistler." I wanted to spit on the ground at the very mention of her name. "I survived her and I'll survive you."

"Brynn who?" She waved this away. "Is she an actress? 'Cause I've never heard of her."

I sat back and watched the soap opera's opening credits.

"Eva?" She sounded curious now.

"I'm not speaking to you," I informed her. "Not until my hair grows back. So get back to me in about two years."

"You're not speaking to me? That is so sweater vest. Ugh." She popped open a can of Red Bull. "You have to speak to me, I'm your roommate."

"My baby-sitting charge," I corrected.

"Oh!" She pretended to be pierced through the heart. "Touché!"

I ignored her.

"Come on, I know the new wardrobe thing was a little immature, but really, you should be down on your knees thanking me: now you know what styles and colors are all wrong for your body."

Ignore, ignore, ignore.

She tried again. "I hear you're going to dinner with Caleb Marx. Can I give you some friendly advice?"

"The last time you gave me friendly advice, I ended up a bald fashion victim."

"Wear a short skirt and put out," she continued, as if I had never spoken. "His mom, like, runs the world. It's worth a few minutes of heavy groping and gold tooth-flavored backwash to be the next Rachel Bilson, *n'est-ce pas?*"

I couldn't think of a reply that wasn't totally sweater vest, so I just kept my mouth shut.

"You're hilarious." She laughed at my stony silence. "So proper. So principled. Well, wait until you've been through a hundred auditions with no callbacks."

"I thought you didn't have that problem," I shot back.

"I don't. But a sweet little thing like you needs all the help she can get. You're pretty, but so is every other girl in the three-one-oh area code. You've got no TV or film experience and you just took your first A and M class this week. Trust me, Nina Marx is a name you *want* in your Sidekick."

"Why do I suddenly feel like I belong on the corner of Hollywood and Vine in a pleather bra and a bad wig?"

"It's not prostitution," she said, sounding eerily like Laurel. "It's networking. Now get over your little hissy fit already. I think Coelle's on the show today and I don't want to miss her."

We didn't have to wait long—a close-up shot of a handsome blond man bemoaning the abduction of his only daughter faded into a scene of our very own Coelle Banerjee, her face artfully smudged with dirt and her black hair disheveled as she struggled to escape her captors in a log cabin in the middle of a forest.

"Hold up. She's supposed to be blondie's *daughter*?" I laughed. "She doesn't look anything like him!"

"Exactly. See, his complexion is a tip-off that she's not really his kid—the mom had an affair with a Colombian drug smuggler while Blondie was in jail for white-collar crimes he didn't commit, but he doesn't know that, so he thinks Hester is his biological child."

"Well, no wonder he got framed, then. He's too dumb to breathe on his own."

"If you're going to be all snotty and scientific, go watch the damn Discovery Channel. I have to see if Hester's dad is going to find out that her mom just flushed the ransom note down the toilet instead of giving it to the police."

"You may break my bones," Coelle yelled onscreen as a burly man in a black ski mask approached, brandishing a baseball bat, "but you'll never break my spirit!"

"So. You're Laurel's niece." Nasih Abicair turned out to be surprisingly soft-spoken, not to mention short and skinny, compared to the vision of the cloven-hoofed, fire-breathing, camera-toting demon I'd conjured up after the discussion with my aunt.

"That's me." I gave him my most winning smile.

He smiled back. "You're very beautiful. I'm sure we'll have a great shoot." And he barely even glanced at my nose. Or my new hair extensions (which I kept trying to convince myself looked *totally natural.*) "Go change, have Nicole do your makeup, and I'll set up here." His studio was filled with the sorts of things I'd always assumed were just used for props on film school infomercials—big, rectangular light boxes, shiny silver reflective plates, giant floor fans.

I spent the next forty-five minutes letting Nicole the makeup artist work her magic. She teased my hair into a tousled, fresh-out-of-bed style and decided I should go with vampy false eyelashes because "your eyes are so big to start with that we might as well play them up."

When she finished with me, I was nothing but a pair of enormous, kohl-rimmed eyes in a tank top. Eva Cordes, the Incredible Walking Retina.

"All right," Nicole said. "You ready to face the dragon?"

But the so-called dragon was still acting perfectly pleasant. He had even turned on some soothing, low-key jazz to help ease me into the shoot. "Lovely," he said. "Just have a seat on the stool, keep your back straight, and turn your shoulders toward me. Excellent."

"Really?" I couldn't help sounding pleased with myself.

"Really. You're a natural!" He started clicking away.

I absolutely marinated in the praise, puckering my lips into what I hoped was a sultry, come-hither moue. This wasn't so bad. Kind of fun, actually. Talk about an easy way to make a living!

I pranced and primped through the next thirty minutes while Nasih encouraged me with things like, "gorgeous!", "stunning!", and "remember who put you on the road to stardom when *Vanity Fair* asks you to be on the cover!".

And then . . . then he put down his camera and took a few steps back. "Hmm," he mused. "Something isn't quite right."

"Is this better?" I asked, tilting my head to one side.

*"Aigh!* No! That makes it worse." His face twisted into a tortured glower. "Your nose. My God, who did your nose?"

"Who . . . did it?" I repeated.

"Yes. Who did it? Your surgeon should be shot."

"Oh, I don't have a surgeon; I was just born this way." Even as I said it, I knew I was walking into a trap.

"Well, that's problem number one right there." He put down the camera, whipped a business card out of his pocket, and practically threw it at me. How? *How* could I have missed the horns, tail, and pitchfork before? "Here is the number of an excellent plastic surgeon on Wilshire. I suggest you give him a call before you subject anyone else to that . . ." he gagged ". . . *appendage.*"

My lower lip started to quiver. "But . . ."

"What's that face about? Are you going to cry?" he barked.

I thought of how much this shoot was costing Aunt Laurel and took a deep, calming breath. "No."

"Good. Because I can't handle even one more hysterical female today. Do you hear me? Not . . . one . . . more."

"I'm not hysterical," I insisted. "I'm calmly accepting some constructive criticism."

"Well, I'm glad to hear that, because there's plenty more where that came from."

And thus began the total nuclear annihilation of my self-esteem. The jazz music was drowned out entirely by his frothy-mouthed critique of my ears ("they stick out"), my thighs ("too scrawny"), my teeth ("crooked on the bottom and you need porcelain veneers"), my knees ("knobby"), my upper arms ("lay off the Cheetos there, pudge"), and, of course, my eyes ("deer caught in the headlights with overdilated pupils"). Also, I seemed to be lacking an overall sense of elegance—"you girls today move like bull elephants." The only thing spared was my chest (and only because "lucky for you, clothes hang better on girls with no breasts").

After another twenty minutes of wielding his camera like a lethal weapon while systematically cataloging my every physical, intellectual, and emotional flaw, Nasih put me out of my misery and declared the session finished.

"I might have gotten one or two decent shots," he said, downloading the images onto the mammoth computer atop his desk. "No thanks to you. If you want to amount to anything, you'll have to learn how to get comfortable in front of a camera."

"Gosh," I murmured. "I can't imagine why that would be a problem."

His irritation veered back to ferocity. "Do you have something to say to me?"

I tried to look meek and guileless. "No."

"Are you *criticizing* me?"

"Of course not." I shook my head so fast, my vision blurred. "I'm just a knock-kneed, scrawny-thighed, big-eyed genetic tragedy trapped in an eighteen-year-old's body."

"That's right." He looked satisfied. "And don't you forget it. I'll e-mail your aunt the best shots of the batch and let her decide what she wants to do, but I urge you to make appointments with a good surgeon, a good nutritionist, and a good dentist, then come back when you're ready to get serious about this."

"Okay." I edged toward the door, relieved that the worst was over. I'd faced the dragon and hadn't shed a tear. Maybe I really was tough enough to make it in this business.

Not so fast.

"You're Marisela Cordes's daughter, right?" he asked as I pulled a cardigan over the crisp white shirt I'd changed into midshoot.

"Mm-hmm."

"Now *there* was a woman who could work the camera. That skin, those lips, and that nose . . . perfection! I was one of the first to work with her. She was the best I ever had," he said dreamily, fondling his camera in a rather pervy manner. "She gave *great* face."

I cleared my throat. "Um . . . good for her?"

"So spontaneous. So instinctive. She knew just how to make the camera fall in love with her." He finally snapped out of his sick little reverie and stared at me. "How on earth did she end up with *you* for a daughter?"

I shrugged.

"Was your father a linebacker or something?"

I shrugged again.

"I'm serious. Did she end up with a pro wrestler or a NASCAR driver or what?"

Oh God. I'd never even considered a pro wrestler. That *would* explain my undisputed reign as arm wrestling champ at Camp Arapaho in seventh grade . . .

"Well?" he snapped.

I heaved a hefty sigh. "I don't know, okay? I don't *know* who my father is."

This shut most people up.

But Nasih was not most people.

"She never told you?" An evil little smirk played on his lips. "Innn-teresting."

I kept my head down and headed for the door. "Thanks for your time."

He chuckled. "Well, given that nose, those teeth, and those shoulders, I'd start my search for Daddy at the international rugby play-offs. Or maybe the alligator-rasslin' tourneys down in Florida."

I escaped out to the parking lot, where the sun was shining, the birds were chirping, and the palm trees were swaying under a perfect blue California sky.

*Then* I started crying.

8

"So you had to do head shots with the Nose Nazi? Did you cry? I knew you would," Jacinda crowed when I returned to the apartment with puffy eyes and a pint of Cold Stone Creamery. "I *knew* you would!"

"Congratulations, you're psychic." I grabbed a soup spoon from the kitchen, then sat down at the table and prepared to dig in. "Throw in a crystal ball and some Tarot cards and you're ready to start your own hotline."

"Are you sure you want to eat that?" Coelle regarded the ice cream with the same revulsion she would a colony of dung beetles. "All that fat, all those calories . . ."

"Just because you never eat doesn't mean we all have to starve. Besides, I'm already pudge-o-rific, according to Nasih, so I might as well enjoy it." I scooped up a huge bite of Mud Pie Mojo.

"Oh, don't let him get to you," she admonished. "Everyone knows he's a sadistic, misogynist narcissist."

"That's a lot of 'ists,'" I muttered between bites.

"You're really going to pollute your system with a tub of refined sugar and cholesterol just because of the Nose Nazi?" Coelle rolled her eyes. "You new girls are so delicate."

"Well, some of us didn't grow up on the set of *Barney*, okay? We can't all be hardened veterans," I shot back. Oh yes. I'd Googled her Oscar-bound ass—*Twilight's Tempest* was only her latest foray into TV infamy. She'd been a *Barney* kid at age five before graduating to guest roles on Nickelodeon and even *90210* (she'd played a hapless hospitalized waif on a very special Christmas episode).

As Jacinda broke out into a rousing chorus of Barney's trademark "I love you, you love me . . . ," Coelle flushed and said, "That was all my mother's doing. And anyway, *I* never cried when producers told me I was too tall or too bucktoothed or too"—she glanced down at her chest—"developed to play a ten-year-old."

Jacinda stopped singing. "But you did cry the first time you did head shots with Nasih."

"I did not! I had allergies!"

"Shut up. You wept like Baby Bop had died in your arms."

"Well, who wouldn't?" I interjected. "The man gave me a referral to an actual plastic surgeon." I whipped out the engraved business card for Dr. Lyle Ankrum.

Coelle glanced at it, then said, "You should hang on to that—he's the best rhinoplasty guy on the West Coast."

I *knew* she'd looked different in the pictures from the *Barney* set. I turned to Jacinda. "What about you?"

She patted her nose. "Not me. I'm all-natural, baby."

"Your *nose* is, anyway." Coelle sniggered.

Jacinda gasped, covered her breasts with her hands, and started in with, "I don't know what you're implying, but if you want to take this outside—"

In an attempt to prevent the ensuing throwdown, I blurted out, "It wasn't just about my nose and my arms and my eyes, though. He went after my dad."

Coelle stopped threatening Jacinda with, "I know where you sleep, principessa," long enough to turn back to me and say, "Your dad? Who's your dad?"

"I don't know," I admitted. "Nasih was explaining how much better my mother was than me, and then he started going on and on about how my father must be, like, a toothless, moonshine-running linebacker."

Coelle finally looked at me with something other than detached disdain. "You really don't know who your own father is?"

"Nope." I picked at the nubby fabric on the couch cushions. "I've had a few hunches over the years, but my mom won't confirm or deny anything. She says it's none of my business."

Jacinda snatched my spoon and helped herself to a big bite of my ice cream. "Uh, hello, I think your dad *is* your business!"

They had momentarily stopped treating me like the Hester Prynne of West Hollywood, so I charged ahead, even though I knew I'd be sorry later. "That's what I keep telling her! I have a right to know, even if only to get a health history—you know, like does breast cancer run in my family, or total insanity—but she says it'll only cause trouble."

"If my mother pulled that, I'd never speak to her again. *And* I'd saw the heels off all her Manolos," Jacinda declared. "That'd be hitting her where it hurts."

"I hardly ever get to speak to her as it is. And I don't live with her, so I don't have shoe access. Besides, it's the only parenting decision she's ever followed through with; she must have a good reason."

"Like what?" Coelle demanded.

"Like my dad has zero interest in getting to know me. Or he's a drug addict. Or in prison. Or remarried to someone younger than I am."

"Ooh! If he's really a fugitive junkie with a taste for cradle robbing, you should track him down and create a reality show," Jacinda said. She'd gone thirty seconds without morphing into a hateful little weasel. A world record. "Family members like that don't come along every day."

"Your compassion is truly touching."

"No, seriously. You shouldn't waste this opportunity. If *my* father were a womanizing thug in the pen, I'd be putting together a series called *Dysfunction Junction* so fast it'd make your head spin." She sighed wistfully. "You're so lucky. Nothing exciting ever happens to me."

Coelle grabbed the ice cream from us, clapped the lid on, and stashed it in the freezer. "Get this away from me. I have a swimsuit scene coming up, remember?"

"Speaking of womanizing thugs." I tried to change the subject without losing their interest. "My dinner date with Caleb Marx is tonight."

"You mean 'C Money'?" Coelle shuddered.

"You mean your ticket to fame and fortune?" Jacinda corrected.

"He's picking me up at seven."

Jacinda crooked one finger to motion me in closer. "Listen, L.A. clubs are infamous for carding—"

*"Infamous,"* Coelle agreed.

"—but I feel a tiny bit bad about what happened to your hair, so I'm going to help you out this one time."

Be afraid. Be very afraid.

"If you want to party, go to Hex. It's the hot new club on San Vicente and they never check ID, especially if you're a gorgeous Allora girl."

"If this is another one of your evil little tricks . . ."

"It's not. Swear to God. My new boyfriend—" She broke off, clapping one hand over her mouth.

Coelle arched a perfectly shaped eyebrow. "Your new boyfriend what?"

"Nothing," she said emphatically. "Especially nothing that Laurel's niece should hear."

"You can tell me," I urged. "I won't tell my aunt, I promise."

"Damn right you won't tell her. Because there's *nothing to tell.*"

"I can keep a secret. Really. I'll put it in the vault," I swore. "Is he a bartender?"

"How insulting. I never sully myself with waitstaff of any kind." She turned to Coelle. "Isn't that true?"

Coelle nodded. "She only sullies herself with brainless male models and waster musicians." She got up from the couch and trudged toward the stairs. "It's been lovely, chicas, but I gotta pack if I'm going to catch my flight. The airport shuttle will be here in forty-five minutes."

"Where are you going?" asked Jacinda, who had missed the mother-daughter screamfest earlier in the week.

Coelle stomped up the stairs. "New York. Tampax commercial. Don't want to talk about it."

"But I thought you were taking that stupid SAT thing on Saturdays?"

"I *said*, I don't want to talk about it." Stomp, stomp, stomp.

"Do you want some dinner before you go?" I called after her. "I just went to the grocery store today. I have tuna and fruit and yogurt and pizza . . ."

Stomp, stomp . . . *slam*.

"Guess she doesn't want to talk about that, either. Toucheee." Jacinda shrugged. "It's all because she never had a real childhood. Her mom is like . . . who's that chick you were talking about before? The biggest bitch in the world?"

"Brynn Kistler?"

"Yeah. Her mom is like Brynn Kistler to the tenth power."

I tried to imagine such a creature. "Wow."

"So tell me, who was this infamous Brynn Kistler and what did she do to drive you all the way across the continental U.S.?"

I just looked at her. "You think we're BFF having a slumber party now, just because you told me where to get booze?"

"Fine. Don't tell me. I don't care anyway, I was just being polite."

"Why don't *you* tell *me* about your new boyfriend?" I countered.

"He's not even officially my boyfriend." She crossed over to the refrigerator and grabbed a Red Bull.

"Then it's no big deal, so you might as well spill."

"He's no one, it's nothing, and that's the end of that story." She chugged her drink and started flipping through the new issue of *InStyle* on the table. "But if I don't happen to make it home tonight, could you do me a favor and cover for me?"

"Why should I cover for you?" I laughed. "You've been a hag and a half to me since the second I walked through the door."

"Then give me an incentive to stop," she shot back. "Cover for me. Laurel doesn't always check up on us, but if she does—"

"Don't try to blackmail me! I'm not covering for you!"

"You'll be sorry if you don't!"

"Why? Because you'll get a lecture from Laurel on the perils of drugs and pregnancy and STDs? You'll have to move out of the apartment and get a new roommate to torture? Stop me when I get to the part where I'll be sorry."

From the expression on her face, it was obvious she didn't hear the word "no" a lot. "The haircut and the clothes were only a warm-up," she hissed.

"Are you threatening me?"

She tossed her hair. "I don't threaten, I deliver."

Why did I suddenly feel like Coelle wasn't the only one trapped in a soap opera? I tossed *my* hair, accepting her challenge. "Do your worst, Crane-Laird. Do your worst."

From: descartesismybizatch@wordup.net <Jeff Oerte>
To: OutOfEden@globecon.com <eva cordes>
Subject: RE: my glamtastic new life
Glad to know your lifelong friends have been replaced after one week in Cali. I'll be sure to say hi to Bryan for you, even though he hasn't mentioned your name once since you left.
He and Brynn are back together and even more vomitously happy than before. ALMOST as vomitously happy as me and Liliana.
Jealous?
J.

From: OutOfEden@globecon.com <eva cordes>
To: descartesismybizatch@wordup.net <Jeff Oerte>
Subject: hot date
Glad to hear things are working out for you and Blondiana. Maybe if you can convince her to go to prom with you, you'll FINALLY get over what happened at homecoming. I myself have a hot date tonight with a guy so gorgeous, so chiseled, so suave that even Abercrombie models are blinded by his man-beauty.
Jealous?
E.

9

The doorbell rang at 7:00 P.M. Twice.

I froze upstairs in the bathroom, mid-lipstick application, and debated turning off all the lights and staying really, really quiet. Maybe he would lose interest and go away.

When the doorbell chimed a third time, I accepted my fate. Caleb Marx might have as few issues with outdated slang and a total lack of street cred, but the boy had persistence.

"Hang on," I called, heading down the stairs. Jacinda had already stormed off to meet up with her mystery man, so I'd have to answer the door and navigate the awkward introductory small talk with no buffer whatsoever.

I paused on the threshold and took a deep breath. Then I grabbed the knob and yanked it open.

"Hi." I pasted on a smile.

"Yo." He greeted me with a quick, unidentifiable hand gesture that he probably thought was a gang symbol. "What's crackin'?"

"Not much." Only four more hours and I'll be free, only four more hours and I'll be free . . . "What's, um, cracking with you?"

"Just crispin', handling my business, you know." He made a big show of shrugging manfully, at which point I noticed he'd gone *way* overboard with the gold chains tonight. Rope upon rope of gold accessorized his shiny black jersey and pristine white Adidas (unlaced—good Lord). Like he just mugged Flava Flav in the parking lot.

"So where would you like to eat?" I asked, assuming the answer would be someplace casual. After all, if he couldn't even be bothered to put on shoelaces . . .

"I got a jones for sushi and sake, so I'm taking us to Saito."

"Fancy." Coelle had mentioned Saito. According to her, it was one of the nicest restaurants in the area.

"Only the best for a babezilla like you. Damn, girl, you look good enough to eat in those jeans."

I gritted my teeth and concentrated on the brunch with my mother that I was going to get out of this. "Thanks. You look pretty sporty yourself."

"I know." He nodded and offered up one scrawny pale arm, complete with a huge, diamond-encrusted watch. When he caught me staring, he grinned and said, "Jacob the Jeweler made it special for me. If you like the good life, you'll love steppin' out with me. One night with Crunk Master C, and you're gonna catch the vapors, guar-an-teed. All the honeys do."

"I'll try to hold myself back." I locked the door behind me and took the arm he offered.

He quickened his pace and dragged me down the block, where his love, his life, his reason for getting up in the morning was waiting.

The gargantuan black Hummer H2 had custom rims, tinted windows, cushy leather seats embroidered with giant silver Cs, and a neon-rimmed license plate reading CRONIC.

When he turned the key in the ignition, I discovered the SUV also had a state-of-the-art sound system with a minimum volume level of "eardrums bleeding."

He didn't open the passenger side door for me, but I managed to scramble in and fasten my seat belt before he peeled away from the curb.

"I gots mad tunes," he informed me, turning the stereo up even louder.

As the bass thrummed through my body, all I could pick out of the lyrics were the words "bitch," "ho," and "hoodrat." Charming.

"Could you turn the music down?" I yelled at the top of my lungs.

"Turn it up? No problem!" And the rhythmic obscenities pumped up even louder.

All this to get a sit-down with the woman who'd given birth to me seventeen years ago? It wasn't fair—all the other bitches, hos, and hoodrats I knew had normal parents who *begged* them to show up to family dinner. Where was the justice?

Given my date's ghetto fabulous attire, I fully expected the hostess at Saito to sneer and give us the "sorry, all our tables are booked" treatment. But no. She immediately recognized him, gushed about how handsome he was getting, made a point of asking after his mother, and seated us in a secluded, candlelit table.

Caleb proceeded to order a round of sake, which I didn't even taste because as far as I could see, the only thing that could make this evening worse would be getting tipsy, letting my guard down, and feeling those spindly fingered, blinged-out hands anywhere on my body. So I stuck with Diet Coke, nibbled my California rolls, and watched my date get absolutely thrashed. No one carded us, no one dared to cut him off, and no one seemed concerned when he started acting like Clay Aiken on crack.

Ugh. Flashbacks to homecoming with Bryan Dufort, when I had said yes to warm beer in his basement and no to the remaining dregs of my dignity.

"Can we go?" I asked after the server cleared our chopsticks and plates.

"No way. I'm gettin' my drink on and I'm feelin' the flow." His gold tooth glinted in the candlelight.

"Don't you think you've had enough?" I wondered aloud when he started on his fifth cup.

"Shut your babblebox. I can slug back a bottle of Remy and not even buzz." He did a chair-dance rendition of the Cabbage Patch and nearly toppled over.

"Obviously." I checked my watch. Ten o'clock. No way was he going to be in any shape to drive tonight. And Jacinda had sworn vengeance and Coelle was on her way to New York . . . "Well, I guess I'll call a cab then."

I tried to catch the server's eye to ask for the number of a taxi company, but Caleb bolted upright and shouted, "We don't need no pansy-ass cab! I got mad driving skillz! Why you always gots to be guzzling the Haterade?" Then he tripped over his chair and collapsed in a heap on the floor.

The entire dining room stopped talking and stared at us while the hostess sprinted over to make sure Nina Marx's son was still breathing.

"Are you okay?" I asked the wriggling mass of gold chains under the table.

"Ow." He stopped writhing around long enough to point an accusatory finger at me. "I think I broke my damn knee. And it's all your fault."

"*My* fault?"

"You and your yapping. Can't a man take the damn edge off without getting hassled to death?"

"Not when he's supposed to drive me home."

"Oh, I get it. You're that kind of girl."

I raised an eyebrow. "The kind that doesn't want to die in a fiery Hummer rollover? Yes, I guess I am."

"It's okay," the hostess whispered. "The manager's calling Danny. He'll drive you both home."

"*Don't call Danny!*" Caleb bellowed.

"Who's Danny?" I asked, hoping that his mom had provided him with a crusty old chauffeur who would prevent any awkward kiss attempts at the end of the evening.

Assuming he was even conscious at the end of the evening.

"No . . . Danny . . ." Caleb slurred, letting a busboy help him to his feet, then staggering off toward the men's room. "Hate that stupid wank."

"Danny's his stepbrother," the hostess said once he was safely out of earshot. "Sometimes we have to call him when

Caleb gets a little too . . . you know. He'll drive you both home."

So he got sloshed here often enough that they actually kept family phone numbers on hand to get him home? What a catch. Maybe for our second date we could get Jacob the Jeweler to design our promise rings.

"We'll get you home, don't worry." The hostess patted my arm.

But she couldn't get me *home* home—home to Massachusetts, where I didn't have to deal with plastic surgery referrals and overcharged credit cards and family members who raised lying and deceit to an art form. Don't get me wrong, Alden had its drawbacks, like, oh, I don't know, the fact that I was a social leper, my former best friend hated me, and I couldn't accept a scholarship to the only college I'd applied to. But still.

If I could turn back time, I'd fill out ten more college applications, spurn Bryan Dufort, and take Jeff seriously when he'd asked me out to homecoming not as a friend. (He'd been laughing maniacally the entire time he did it, so I'd kind of assumed he was kidding.)

But no. I was stuck in the here and now, waiting for an anemic West Side roller to finish puking in the bathroom of the trendiest sushi joint in town so his stepbrother—who apparently had nothing better to do on a Friday night than sit home and wait for Saito's call—could drive me back to a hostile and possibly armed old-money debutante.

After another fifteen minutes, the waiters started to drop pointed hints about how they needed to seat new diners in our booth. So I paid for dinner with the credit card of doom, slunk over to the bar, and nursed a glass of cranberry juice followed by a big icy chaser of homesickness.

Just as I was about to give up on the elusive Danny and walk home through the dark streets of West Hollywood in three-and-and-half-inch heels, I saw him. Striding through the glass doors, threading his way through the crowd of black-leather-jacketed hipsters, was my knight in shining armor (okay, a UCLA sweatshirt and a baseball cap).

He glanced at the bartender, who nodded in my direction. I had twenty seconds to straighten my shoulders and check my teeth for lipstick residue before he arrived at my side.

"You're Eva?" His eyes were a warm, friendly brown.

"I'm Eva."

"I'm Danny." He offered up a handshake and I slipped my fingers into his.

He stopped smiling and stared at me. And not a scary, serial killer stare. More like a hormones-gushing, sparks-a-flyin' stare.

I stared right back, forgetting to be self-conscious about my pudgy upper arms and my Precious Moments eyes.

Maybe I *wasn't* so sorry I'd left Massachusetts and moved three thousand miles on a whim. Score one for Hollywood.

# 10

"So . . ." Danny let go of my hand and started jangling his keys.

"So . . ." I tried to think of something fascinating and hilarious to say.

"Where is the little lush, anyway?"

"Who?" I blinked. "Oh, C Mon—I mean, Caleb."

He nodded. "Yeah. Your date? Remember him?"

I pointed toward the restroom. "Last time I saw him, he was headed that-a-way."

"That kid is such a lightweight." He rolled his eyes. "Back in a minute."

And he was, half carrying a bleary-eyed C Money.

"Let's go." He started toward the front door. "My car's parked around the corner."

His car turned out to be an ancient diesel Mercedes, not nearly as ostentatious as the Hummer but blissfully free of beatbox-backed pimp anthems.

Working together, we crammed Caleb into the back. Then we settled into the front seat and looked at each other.

"Do I even want to know how many times you've had to come out here to make sake runs?" I asked.

"No." He grinned. "But it's okay. One of my roommates is an aspiring opera singer—I didn't know this until he started in with the vocal warm-ups and the scales in the bathroom at *six thirty every morning*—so I got to escape the world's most tedious choir concert to come down here."

"An opera singer, huh? Does he go around in a cape and a tux, looking tortured?"

"No, it's more like his secret identity. He's probably the only biochem major in the world who sings Wagner while he's blowing stuff up with hydrochloric acid." He paused. "Don't take this the wrong way, but you seem a little too . . . coherent to be going out with C Money."

"Oh, I'm not," I said emphatically. "No. This is strictly a one-time thing. It was sort of a blind date. Against my will. Gone horribly wrong."

"So you wouldn't say he's your boyfriend?"

"God, no." I glanced toward the backseat, where Caleb had dozed off, his gold chains jingling softly when he inhaled. "I'm a free agent." I tried to decide how far I could push this without verging into over-eager desperation. "Totally single."

But all he said was, "Oh." Hmph.

I instructed him to take a right on Waring, and tried again. "What about you? Do you have a girlfriend?"

"Nope."

"What an amazing coincidence." Okay. I had officially verged. Time to shut up and let him make the next move.

"But . . ." He cleared his throat. "You probably don't date college guys."

"Sure I do! I already finished high school so, you know, we're practically classmates."

"You're in college?"

"I'm kind of taking some time off. I got accepted early admission to Leighton, but then I had a change of plans because, well, it's a long story, but the point is, I just moved out here from Massachusetts."

For a few moments, the only sound was Caleb's raspy breathing. Then Danny asked, "Have you been to the beach yet?"

"No, and I haven't had a single celebrity sighting, either. What's up with that? I thought you couldn't order a Frappucino at Starbucks without tripping over Cameron Diaz or Tobey Maguire."

"Try the Coffee Bean and Tea Leaf. That's the local independent coffeehouse chain."

"Well, where is it? I need to stake it out so I can tell my former best—" I stopped myself so I wouldn't have to get into the whole, sordid saga "—my friends from home that I'm mingling with the rich and famous."

"If you really want to see some stars, you should just go to a movie premiere."

"Yeah, but first I have to get *cast* in a movie."

"No, you don't." He suddenly got all twitchy. "I get premiere passes from my stepmother all the time. In fact, she gave me two tickets for this new Rob Marshall movie. I was just gonna give them to my roommate and his girlfriend, but if you . . . you know . . ."

I held my breath while trying to look sophisticated and blasé.

" . . . If you might be interested in going, maybe we could . . ."

"I can't wait!" Note to self: work on sophisticated and blasé routine. "Oh, turn left at the STOP sign."

"Okay, the premiere's on Wednesday night, so if you give me your phone number . . ." Even in the darkness, I could tell he was turning red. "Or just your e-mail, if you want . . ."

My smile faded as I realized we had reached our destination. "Pull over here. My building's the one on the right with all the rosebushes."

I dug through my expensive new purse until I came up with a pen and a gum wrapper, on which I scribbled the apartment phone number and my e-mail address. "What am I supposed to wear to this premiere, anyway? It's, like, sequins and ballgowns, right?" Back to the mall with Laurel's credit card. I'd just tell her that was the price of networking.

"Only if you're A-list. The regular people just wear black. Black jackets, black pants, black shoes."

"So I should just pretend I'm dressing for a funeral?"

"Or you're in the Secret Service," he said, pocketing the scribbled-on gum wrapper I handed to him.

"Okay." I felt like little cartoon hearts and bluebirds were circling my head. "See you Wednesday."

Swoon! Thank God I'd been strong-armed into going out with Nina Marx's horrible little demon spawn.

Speaking of whom . . .

"Erg . . ." Our extra baggage in the backseat lurched back into consciousness. "What the . . . Danny?"

Danny glanced into the rearview mirror. "Welcome back to the Hangover Hilton. Will you be checking in?"

Caleb smacked the back of his seat. "I can't believe that stupid table jockey called your punk ass."

"I should go." I reached for the door handle.

The sound of my voice apparently reminded him that he had, at some point, enjoyed female companionship this evening. "Wait . . . baby . . . where you running off to so fast?"

A long, freckled arm flopped over the seatback and started pawing at my neck and shoulders.

I lunged into the cool night air as Danny reached into the backseat and started pummeling his stepbrother.

"'Bye!" I called, safely out of groping distance. "I had an . . . unusual time."

"You're going home?" Caleb slurred. "But the party's just getting started!"

Danny and I ignored him and stared at each other for another moment.

*Call me,* I mouthed at him.

"I will!" C Money yowled. "I put your digits on speed dial, boo!"

I glided into the apartment on flirtation-fueled clouds of bliss. I might not believe in love at first sight, but I definitely believed in hotness at first sight, and Danny was it.

And tomorrow morning, I'd finally get to see my mom.

# 11

I woke up early Saturday morning to prep for the big brunch. Laurel had made reservations at the Ivy, which, according to Coelle, was *the* place to see and be seen. Before I even hit the bathroom, I checked Jacinda's room to see if she'd come back last night.

Her bed was empty. Correction: she'd stuffed a bunch of lumpy pillows and a giant ski parka under her sheets in a truly lame attempt to fool the casual observer; I spotted the ruse from halfway down the hall. Pathetic. An eighth grader breaking curfew could have done better.

While I showered, I prayed my aunt would ask where Jacinda was so I could get her tiny, designer-encased butt evicted. Then I selected my outfit. I wanted to wear something my mom would appreciate. Translation: something I'd never normally wear.

While I sucked in my stomach and yanked up the zipper to my new Great China Wall jeans—I figured I'd pair them with my new silver Celine sandals and a bright pink cashmere off-the-shoulder sweater I'd ordered online when I first found out I was coming to L.A. because it had looked like something my mom would buy—I thought about Danny.

He was so nice. So cute. So different from, ahem, certain boys at my old school. When he'd wanted to ask me out, he'd come right out with it. No passing notes in study hall. No maniacal laughter. No using me as a booty pawn to get back at his vindictive girlfriend. He'd even agreed to bail out his punky little stepbrother, even though Caleb clearly didn't deserve it. Yes, Danny was a member of a semifunctional family, something I could only dream about.

Right on cue, there was a knock at the front door. Mom.

I flung open the door, ready to greet the woman I hadn't seen in three years and came face-to-face with . . . Laurel?

"Hi." My aunt's voice sounded like she'd been up all night chain smoking. Her expression was grim, without a trace of a smile.

"Hi." I leaned forward, trying to peer down the walkway behind her without being too obvious.

"She's not here, pet." Uh-oh. Her eyes were all awash with pity again.

"Oh." I couldn't believe how disappointed I felt. *Why* did I never learn? Why did I keep expecting her to morph into some wry but nurturing maternal goddess straight out of *Gilmore Girls*? I was supposed to be *smart*.

Aunt Laurel squeezed my shoulder. "Oh God, don't look like that."

"Like what?"

"Like you're a kitten who's about to get stuffed in a blender. We're still having brunch with your mom, we're just not going to the Ivy."

I tried to look nonchalant. "Okay. Great. Where are we going?"

"My house. Marisela said it would be cozier and easier to catch up if we just stayed home."

"Okay. That's cool."

She narrowed her eyes. "But I have never known your mother to turn down a meal at the Ivy. Especially one that I'm paying for."

"You think she has an ulterior motive?" I asked wearily.

"Always."


Take *The OC,* multiply by *Cribs,* mix in Caesers Palace casino, and add just a splash of Buckingham Palace—that's what my aunt's house looked like. An ornate wrought-iron gate opened to a gently sloped green lawn and a grand portico with marble stairs leading up to massive teak doors. Laurel parked in the circular driveway and led me into the foyer, which featured a soaring ceiling, a huge mural of a Tuscan vineyard, and a gigantic crystal chandelier that would kill me instantly if it fell. Plus gold trim. A *lot* of gold trim. Like Donald Trump had been the interior decorator.

"The previous owner had a thing for Italy," she explained when she caught me staring at the mural. "He was an action hero star with a lot more money than taste."

"It's not so bad," I lied, unable to tear my gaze away from the garish grapevines and barefoot peasant workers.

"Please. I retch every time I walk in the door." She tossed her purse onto a glass-topped side table and indicated that I should do the same. "But I haven't had time to call the painters. I'm a busy woman, you know."

"I know."

"Mari?" Laurel's voice echoed off the marble floor. "We're back."

No reply.

"Mari?" Laurel stepped into the living room while I checked the hall.

"Maybe she couldn't take the pressure of seeing me again and ran off to Rodeo Drive," I suggested. "That's what happened last time she visited Massachusetts—after forty-eight hours trapped in the house with Grandma, she freaked out and spent the rest of the trip at the outlet mall."

Laurel shook her head. "Nah, I confiscated her car keys before I left."

"You had to *ground* her to force her to have brunch with me?"

"I just like to cover all the bases, pet." She froze, then raised her chin, sniffing. "Do you smell that?"

I could barely discern the scent that permeated my earliest childhood memories—Virginia Slims Menthol Lights. "Cigarettes?"

"Mm-hmmm." She started up the spiral staircase. "Dammit, I told her eighty thousand times not to smoke in my house."

I trailed after her, my stomach churning with dread and anticipation.

Laurel charged straight into the master suite—an extravaganza of heavy white brocade, gold leaf, and a black velvet dog bed embroidered with HIS NIBS—where we found the double doors leading to the walk-in closet flung open.

"No!" My aunt clapped her hand over her mouth. "She wouldn't dare!"

But that was the thing about my mom: she *always* dared. And she never cared who she pissed off in the process.

"Marisela!" Laurel's voice strangled in rage.

"Back so soon?" My mother's voice was sweet and slow with a bit of a lilt. "Come on in."

The walk-in closet was about twice the size of my bedroom. The pristine white walls housed racks of color-coded clothes, shelves lined with designer shoes, and cubbies stuffed with leather purses. A white armchair sat in the corner, next to a sleek chest of drawers to hold jewelry and lingerie.

And smack dab in the middle, surrounded by all this order and methodical beauty, was my mother. Wearing high heels, a diamond necklace, a red lace thong, and nothing else.

"Oh my God." Laurel grabbed my shoulders and steered me back toward the bedroom. "Cover your eyes."

"Don't be so Victorian," Mom admonished her. "Evie, baby, it's so good to see you!" She stepped forward to engulf me in a bear hug, which I couldn't bring myself to return. "Oh, how I've missed you!"

"I've . . . missed you, too," I managed. I had wanted to see my mother. Just not *so much* of her.

"Would you please cover yourself?" Laurel snatched up a fluffy white bathrobe and tossed it at Mom.

"Relax, babe. Eva's seen me naked before."

"Yeah, when she was born! Don't you have any dignity?"

"I'm gorgeous, I don't need dignity. I work hard for this body, I paid good money for this magnificent rack, and I will not hide my light under a burka."

Even though I was probably scarred for life now, I had to admit she looked good. Her long black hair was curled to perfection (she was fanatical about her hair—it looked like a shampoo ad even in the photos Laurel had taken while she was in the maternity ward after having me), her lips looked freshly collagened, and though her face seemed thinner and kind of strained, she still had her trademark supermodel pout. This, combined with her long legs, toned stomach, and gravity-defying boobs (seriously, would it *kill* her to strap on a bra?), made her look like Janice Dickinson's younger sister.

"We've all seen your silicone rack now." Laurel snarled. *"Put something on."*

Her eyes lit up when she noticed my outfit. "Ooh, I love that sweater. And those shoes! Look at her, Laurel, my little baby's turning into a fashion plate." She started in with the nude hugging again. "I'm so glad to see you! *Mwah! Mwah!* Can I try on your top?"

She started peeling it off me while Laurel assessed the damage. "Have you been trying on my evening gowns?"

"Well, *you* never wear them." She yanked the neck hole of the sweater over my head. "They're just moldering away in here."

I surrendered the sweater, then covered myself with the white bathrobe.

"And my jewelry!" Laurel stabbed an accusatory finger at

Mom's neck. "Take that off this instant! That is a genuine Neil Lane!"

"I have excellent taste." Mom tugged my sweater down over her hips and strutted over to the full-length mirror. "Ooh, this clashes with my thong."

"Then put on some pants!" Laurel yelled. "And stop smoking in here!"

"Bossy, bossy." Mom winked at me, snatched a pair of shiny black dominatrix pumps from the shoe rack, and shoved her feet in.

"You're going to stretch out my shoes!" My aunt yelped as she raced around hanging up clothes, stubbing out cigarettes, returning earrings to their velvet boxes. "I will kill you for this, Mari, do you hear me? I will—wait a minute, what's that noise?"

We all froze for a moment, listening to the muffled growling from behind the sofa.

"Oh, that's just Rhett." Mom selected a ruffled pink chiffon skirt. "He's keeping me company. My furry little style consultant."

"Nooo," Laurel keened as the black poodle emerged from his hiding place, dragging a mangled Chanel handbag. *"Nooo!"*

"Oopsie," Mom said mildly, nodding at her reflection. "Guess he's not a fan of Karl Lagerfeld." She grinned at me again. "Doesn't this sweater look hot on me? I bet none of your friends' mothers can fit into their daughters' clothes."

"I don't have any friends," I muttered.

"And I love your hair. It looks just like mine!"

"It's fake," I said. "Extensions."

Laurel wrestled the purse from the canine jaws of death and herded us toward the bedroom. "Everyone out, out, *out*."

"Fine. Spoilsport." Mom threaded her arms through mine like we were old shopping buddies. "So what's new at school?"

"I left in disgrace." I stumbled over the hem of the bathrobe.

"So did I." She laughed, letting her perfect hair cascade back over her perfect shoulders. "High school is such a waste of time. A penal colony for the terminally banal."

"You're going to pay for that purse," Laurel informed her as we started down the stairs. "And the dry cleaning for all of my suits that now reek of tobacco."

"Whatever you say. What's for brunch?"

"You're unbelievable."

"Why? Because I'm hungry?"

My mom and my aunt stared each other down in a wordless battle of wills.

"You're going to ingest something besides caffeine and nicotine? Fine. *Fine.* We'll have a lovely brunch in the dining room, assuming you can keep your clothes on that long. I'll tell Veronica we're ready to eat." Laurel stalked off toward the kitchen, but her tone warned that this fight was not over.

"Come sit down with me in the living room." Mom tugged me toward a pristine tan leather sofa. "I want to hear everything about everything—your trip, your apartment, your new boyfriend . . ."

"I don't have a boyfriend." *Yet,* I added silently, starting to smile as my thoughts turned to Danny yet again.

"Don't play coy with me! Laurel told me all about you and the casting director's son. What was his name?"

My smile disappeared. "Caleb Marx, a.k.a. C Money?"

"Yeah, the rap guy."

"No, no." My dangly silver earrings whapped my cheeks as I shook my head. "He's not a rap guy and he's *definitely* not my boyfriend. I went out with him once, but only because I had no choice."

"Why didn't you have any choice?"

Because I wanted to see you, you self-absorbed, chain-smoking, child-neglecting, sweater-swiping nudist. "Never mind. The point is, we had one horrible date and now we're through."

She looked dubious. "That's not what Laurel said."

"Yeah, well, she's not the one who had to suffer through dinner with him."

She fingered the diamond choker around her neck. "So what else is going on with you?"

I thought of everything that had happened in the last three years, all the highs and lows and firsts and lasts that I'd been planning to recount (in amusing, bite-size anecdotes, of course). Then I thought about her looking at her own reflection in the closet mirror instead of at me and decided not to tell her anything. "Not much."

She nodded. We both gazed at the plush off-white carpet on the living room floor. The seconds ticked by on a towering grandfather clock in the corner. Three years and three thousand miles and we had absolutely nothing to say to each other. What a waste of frequent flyer miles this trip turned out to be.

"Well?" She finally rallied. "Aren't you going to ask me how I've been?"

I shrugged one shoulder. "How've you been?"

"Wrecked. Ravaged. Ruined by love." She collapsed back against the sofa cushions. "I gave up New York and London and St. Tropez to come back here and start a new life. I finally found a man to give my heart to, I thought he was my soul mate, but . . ." She inhaled, long and shuddery. "We were torn apart by lies and spiteful gossip."

"You had a fight with that guy? Tyson O'Donnell?" Not that I had memorized the entire G-Spot item or anything.

"That bitch Gigi Geltin always had it in for me." Her eyes welled up. "Do you have any tissues?"

I checked the bathrobe's pockets. "Nope. Sorry."

She grabbed my robe's terry-cloth sleeve and blotted her smeary mascara. "That rumor-mongering harpy has hated me since leg warmers were cool. Just because one of the guys from Def Leppard broke up with her to spend the summer with me in the south of France. And now I'm a prisoner in my own home."

Laurel's own home, actually, but I let that one slide. "Wait. Why are you a prisoner? Why couldn't we have brunch at the Ivy?"

She wiped her nose on my sleeve. Ew. "Because people might see us at the Ivy. People I know."

"So what?"

"Well, I hate to ruin our big reunion, but I have something to tell you. Now don't get upset until I finish, okay?"

"Okay," I said slowly, trying to strap on my emotional crash helmet.

"I didn't want to go to the Ivy with you because I don't want people to know I'm your mother."

Why didn't she just reach over and punch me in the face?

"Wait, hang on a second, baby girl, don't get upset."

"Too late," I choked out.

She tugged a lock of my hair. "Oh, Evie, why do you always assume the worst about me? I love you more than anything in the world. On any other day, I'd take you out and show you off and buy you your first mimosa. But Tyson and I had a huge fight last night over that stupid, libelous gossip column and I don't want to give him any more reasons to be mad at me."

"Why would my being here make him mad?" I crossed my arms. "Doesn't he want to meet your kid?"

"Not exactly." She pasted on a fake, dopey grin. "It's more like he doesn't know I *have* a kid."

# 12

"Oh my God." I leapt up from the sofa. "You didn't tell your boyfriend I exist?"

"Of course he knows you exist. I mean, give me a little credit, baby girl, I've got pictures of you plastered all over. I always have at least one in my suitcase when I travel—framed and everything!" She cleared her throat. "And actually, he's not my boyfriend, he's my fiancé. At least, he *was* my fiancé until Gigi Geltin screwed me over. Anyway, when he saw the photos of you, he just assumed you were my little sister. And I never corrected him and now . . . well, it would be kind of awkward to tell him right now."

"Why the hell would he assume I'm your sister?"

She twisted her hands together. "Well, when I met him, I kind of shaved a few years off my age."

"How many years?"

"Five."

I glared at her.

"Okay, ten. It's a lady's prerogative to lie about her age."

"But it is *not* a lady's prerogative to lie about her daughter!"

"I know, and I feel awful, just sick about the whole thing." She extended both hands toward me. "I promise I'll tell him everything as soon as we get the engagement back on track, but right now we're on shaky ground and I don't want him to think he can't trust me."

"Well, he *can't* trust you!" I exploded. "No one can trust you!"

Her face paled. "How can you say that?"

"You're the most untrustworthy human being on the planet. You say you miss me? Lie. You say you care what's going on in my life? Lie. You say you love me? Lie!"

"I do love you, sweetheart—"

"Stop it!" My palms itched to seize one of the thick-walled crystal vases and smash it against the fireplace. "You don't love me; you won't even admit I'm your child!"

She stretched her arms up, hoping we could hug it out. "Don't be like this, Eva. I'm trying as hard as I can—"

"Forget it." I turned my back on her. "I'm going home. Enjoy your new sweater, *Mother.*"

"What's going on?" Aunt Laurel had returned from the kitchen.

"Nothing!" my mom said quickly, lowering her arms. "Just a little mother-daughter chat. We're, um, bonding."

I strode into the foyer. "I'm leaving. Right now."

"Don't let her go." Mom rushed up behind me. "I know you're upset, but honestly, if you'd give me just two minutes to explain . . ."

I turned to Laurel. "If you don't want to drive me back to the apartment, can you at least tell me which bus to take?"

My aunt shook her head at my mom. "I can't leave you alone for a minute."

"I didn't do anything!" she protested, the very picture of wronged innocence. "All I said was—"

I clutched my purse strap in both hands, still wearing the bathrobe over my jeans. "I'm out of here. Right now. Is someone going to give me a ride or do I have to walk back to West Hollywood?"

"Don't get dramatic," Laurel said. "I'll drive you."

"Thank you."

"I am not through talking to you, young lady!" my mom sputtered.

I reached for the doorknob.

She gasped and stomped her high heels against the marble floor. "Eva Cordes, don't you dare walk out that door!"

Not only did I walk out, I slammed it.

Laurel offered to take me to brunch at the Ivy, just the two of us, but I wasn't really in the mood for pancakes and freshly squeezed orange juice anymore. And the bathrobe wasn't exactly paparazzi-friendly.

I checked our voice mail as soon as I entered the apartment, hoping that Danny had called, and—woo hoo!—we had one new message.

But the voicemail wasn't from Danny: "Yo, boo . . ."

*Nooo!*

". . . last night was poppin' for real. Well, except for when that naggly fool Danny showed up. That was cold swaggish. But forget that. We're going out galavantin' again this week. You're my new gambo, girl. And hey, my mom says she's casting a new WB pilot next week, so send her a head shot, yo, and we'll hook your sweet ass *up*."

Welcome to the casting couch. Ick, ick, ick.

"Holla back at me tonight and we'll crisp, aiight?"

WTF? Did they do a special language arts course called I Wanna Be a Hip-Hop Playa at his prep school?

I heard the jangle of keys, then Jacinda tumbled in the front door. She looked like I felt: makeup smeared all over her face, hair sticking out at odd angles, one shoe missing.

"What a night!" She breezed by me and stuck her head into the refrigerator. "I've got to cool down."

She was wearing the same purple halter top and black leather pants she'd had on last night.

I took a long look at her, turned on my heel, and headed upstairs.

"Hey!" she yelled after me. "I broke curfew! Aren't you going to smack my hand with a ruler?"

I kept going and threw myself down on my bed.

"Eva?" She leaned into the open doorway, pressing an icy can of diet soda against her forehead. "Hello? Here I am, resident girl gone wild. Time to ground me, right?"

I pressed my face into the pillow. "I couldn't care less what—and who—you've been doing all night."

"Really?" She sounded disappointed. "What happened to you?"

"Nothing."

"Oh, *something* definitely happened." She barged right in and gave me an expectant look. "I thought you were planning to bludgeon me with your blow-dryer. Seriously, what gives? And what is this avant-garde ensemble about?" She tugged on the bathrobe belt.

"I had brunch with my aunt and my mom." Horrifyingly, my voice got all high-pitched and squeaky as I said this. "Well, I tried to have brunch with them."

"What happened?"

"Nothing. Leave me alone."

"Oh, come on, you can tell me. What happened? A little mama drama? I know all about that." I felt the mattress dip as she sat down next to my feet.

"No, you don't. Trust me."

"Well, then, enlighten me."

"I'm not giving you any more ammunition to use against me. How stupid do you think I am?"

"I *said* I was sorry for the haircut and the gauche style picks."

"And what about the death threats last night?"

She twisted her tangled blond hair up into a messy topknot. "Please. I would never waste my time killing a nobody like you. If I'm going to prison, it'll be for brawling with an A-lister. Like Keira Knightley—I wouldn't mind feuding with her."

I pulled the bathrobe tighter around me. "Bye."

"Oh, don't get all whiny and weak sauce. I know I've been a bit of a—what was her name?"

"Brynn Kistler," I supplied.

"—Brynn Kistler lately, but it's only because I was bored. And I don't like to share the bathroom."

"And you've got a sadistic streak a mile wide."

She frowned. "I do not. I was just finding out if you were as cream puff as you looked."

"Well, you win," I spat. "Because I'm leaving. I'm not going to waste any more of my life in this stupid, superficial city."

"Then you might as well tell me everything. I can be supportive as hell—you'll see. Besides, *Twilight's Tempest* isn't on today, and I need my daily dose of scandal. Hit me."

So I did. I told her every sordid detail about brunch, from the red thong to the white bathrobe. All the pent-up fury and frustration boiled over, and while I ranted and raved and pounded the pillow for emphasis, Jacinda just sat and stared.

Finally, I settled down enough to let her get a word in edgewise. ". . . And that's why I'm never speaking to my mother again."

"Jeez. You're not so sweater vest after all." She looked at me with newfound respect. "What are you going to do about all this?"

I shrugged. "What *can* I do except move on and accept the fact that she's never going to be mom material?"

A diabolical grin twisted the corners of her mouth. "You can get revenge. She can't treat you like that and get away with it!"

"That's your job," I said dryly.

"She won't tell you who your father is, she won't even acknowledge she's your mother. She's turned you into an orphan! You don't have to take that."

"I know, but—"

"Why should you pretend you were never born just so she can marry some random jackhole? Don't let her walk all over you!"

"But the thing is—"

"No 'buts'. If she's not going to be a good mom, you don't have to be a good daughter!"

Her outrage fueled mine like gasoline on a fire. "Yeah! Why should I always have to suffer in silence?"

"Exactly. You're mad as hell and you're not going to take it anymore!"

"That's right!"

"She wants to deny your existence? You'll show her!"

"Damn straight!" I paused. "Wait. How am I going to show her?"

"You're going to be all over her like gin on tonic. By the time we're finished, she'll understand that Eva Cordes will not be ignored."

From: descartesismybizatch@wordup.net <Jeff Oerte>
To: OutOfEden@globecon.com <eva cordes>
Subject: Saturday night
So how was your date with Rico Suave?


From: OutOfEden@globecon.com <eva cordes>
To: descartesismybizatch@wordup.net <Jeff Oerte>
Subject: RE: Saturday night
Great. How was your date with the bimbo? Did she paint my old bedroom lavender with unicorns? She sounds like the type.


From: descartesismybizatch@wordup.net <Jeff Oerte>
To: OutOfEden@globecon.com <eva cordes>
Subject: RE: RE: Saturday night
I don't know what her bedroom looks like, but I'll be finding out very soon, if last night was any indication.


From: OutOfEden@globecon.com <eva cordes>
To: descartesismybizatch@wordup.net <Jeff Oerte>
Subject: RE: RE: RE: Saturday night
You slut.

From: descartesismybizatch@wordup.net <Jeff Oerte>
To: OutOfEden@globecon.com <eva cordes>
Subject: (no subject)
I'm a slut? I could say a lot of things right now about you and Bryan Dufort, but I won't.


From: OutOfEden@globecon.com <eva cordes>
To: descartesismybizatch@wordup.net <Jeff Oerte>
Subject: Saturday night
I take it back—you're not a slut, you're a pig. Well, toodles, dahling, I'm off to go club hopping with my NEW best friend, Jacinda Crane-Laird. (Yes, THAT Jacinda Crane-Laird.) Then tomorrow I'll probably go shopping with my mother. She and I are totally bonding—it's a regular mom-a-palooza out here. Leaving MA was the best decision I ever made.


From: descartesismybizatch@wordup.net <Jeff Oerte>
To: OutOfEden@globecon.com <eva cordes>
Subject: RE: Saturday night
"Toodles"? Could you tell the REAL Eva Cordes to give me a call when you find her?

# 13

I agreed to let Jacinda do my makeup for our big night out, which, considering her obsession with fake eyelashes and crimson lipstick, was quite a leap of faith.

"Don't go overboard," I cautioned. "Keep it tasteful."

"Tasteful is overrated." She slathered green shadow on my eyelids. "If you want people to notice you, you have to stand out from the crowd."

I shifted around on the rim of the porcelain bathtub. "But I don't want people to notice me because I look like a ho."

"Haven't you ever heard the saying, There's no such thing as bad publicity?" She took a step back, frowned, then grabbed a tube of mascara. "If people are talking about you, you're somebody. If they aren't talking about you, you're nobody. Simple."

"And wearing three coats of mascara is going to get people talking about me?" I asked dubiously.

"No. Being seen at a club opening with *me* is going to get people talking about you. And I don't want word to get out that I have hicktown, nonglam friends. Anyway, if you don't look stunning, no one's going to reprint the photos of us in the magazines. They'll make you step out of the picture and just shoot me, and then our plan won't work."

"Yeah, about that." I winced as she attacked my eyebrows with tweezers. "I've been thinking about this and I'm not so sure the plan's really as genius as we originally thought. You don't know my mom. She's gonna have a meltdown. Like, seriously, big-time, full-on, check-herself-into-a-mental-institution meltdown."

"So? Who cares?" She broke out the lip gloss. "Let her check in. Sounds like she's way overdue."

"True." I quashed the twinges of guilt that had started to seep into my anger. "She needs a reality check. Not to mention a lobotomy."

"Exactly. You don't have to play the victim forever."

When I glanced in the mirror, I was startled to see that Jacinda's makeup job made me look like I was at least twenty-three. "Wow."

"See? You're too hot to be worrying about things like other people's feelings. No one likes a martyr," she said firmly. "But everyone likes a gorgeous Allora girl. We are going to be the talk of the town!"

• • •

"How did you get invited to this thing, anyway?" I asked as Jacinda gunned her silver Mercedes convertible down La Cienega Boulevard.

"Ask me no questions, I'll tell you no lies." She floored it through a freshly red light.

"What does that mean?"

"It means you don't want to know."

At Jacinda's urging, I had managed to squeeze myself into one of her cocktail dresses (a short, lacy Collette Dinnigan number) while she opted for skintight jeans, a green satin top with a neckline cut down to her navel, and a real emerald necklace.

"All you need to know is that Gigi Geltin mentioned the Troika Club opening in today's G-Spot. She said it's VIPs only, and you know what that means."

"We can't get in?"

"Press galore. Photographers, gossip columnists, party crashers . . . all the things I love about L.A." She cut off a sedan, screeched around the corner, and barreled down a dark alley. I covered my eyes.

"I can't wait till I start getting big, juicy movie roles," she went on. "Then I can make some real bank and I won't be at the mercy of my parents. This car is *two years old* and they won't let me trade it in for a new one! It's so humiliating. I want to get a Maybach, but they're all, 'those are noveau riche.' And I can't touch my trust fund until my twenty-fifth birthday, so—"

"Jacinda!" I yelped as a cat streaked across the alley. "Watch the road!"

"My mom lives in Manhattan; if I need a defensive driving

lecture, I'll call her." She vroomed out of the alley, turned right without even tapping the brakes, blew through a STOP sign, and pulled up to a crowded valet station. "God. Talk about eighteen going on eighty." She tossed her keys to the valet, grabbed my wrist, and tugged me into the frantic mob of people clogging the sidewalk. "Are you ready for your first red carpet appearance?"

"Uh . . ."

"Just remember: stay close to me, angle one shoulder forward, turn your hips to the side so you look thinner, don't smile too wide, and try not to blink." She shoved her way through to a sour-faced woman with a clipboard, three cellphones, and a headset.

"Jacinda!" The woman's face lit up as soon as she saw us. "I'm delighted you could make it."

Jacinda handed over her invitation and tapped the clipboard. "I should be on the list."

"Of course, sweetie, come right in. Enjoy! Wilmer and Leo are already at the bar."

"Stellar." Jacinda yanked me forward. "And this is my new roommate, Eva Cordes. She's going to be the next big thing. Eva, this is Patsy Thockmorton, publicist extraordinaire."

"Hi, sweetie." Patsy gave me a totally insincere smile. "Any friend of Jacinda's . . ."

Jacinda tugged my hand again and we tumbled through to the gauntlet of photographers.

"Stop blinking," she hissed as I instinctively raised an arm to ward off the blinding flood of flashbulbs. "And put your hand down!"

"I can't see!"

"You don't need to see! Shut up and pose!"

And I tried. But between the yelling ("Jacinda! Look over here!", "Jacinda! Show us some boob!", "Jacinda! Turn to the left!") and the flashbulbs, it was all I could do to remain upright. Why didn't anyone *warn* me that working the red carpet was like trying to skateboard at the X Games in stilettos? Drunk?

Then the photographers turned on me like rabid wolverines. "Who's that nobody?", "She's ruining my pictures!", "Hey, chickie, get out of the photo! Jacinda alone!"

Finally, Jacinda stopped batting her eyelashes at the photographers and introduced me.

"Gentlemen, this is my friend Eva and you'll want to keep her in your photos."

"No, I won't!" someone hollered. "I gotta sell these to *People,* and *People* doesn't care about some beautiful, anonymous hanger-on!"

"Hey!" I protested, but Jacinda shot me a warning glance.

"This is Eva," she purred to the press. "Eva Cordes. C-O-R-T—"

"D," I corrected. "C-O-R-D-E-S."

"And she's not a hanger-on. She's practically Hollywood royalty. Her mother is . . ." She turned to me, muttering, "What's your mom's name again?"

"Marisela Cordes," I supplied. "That's M-A-R-I-S—"

"We know who Marisela is," they chorused. "Eighties' supermodel has-been!"

"Well, I'm her daughter."

"I didn't know Marisela had a kid," a photographer said, snapping away at us.

"It's been a very juicy secret all these years," Jacinda cooed. "But now the truth is out and Eva's going to be a white-hot star."

Then someone asked the inevitable question, the question I should have known was coming, the question guaranteed to launch me out of obscurity and into the gossip columns: "Who's your dad, Eva?"

"I . . . he . . . I . . ." I stammered, flushing from head to toe.

"Hey! We don't got all night, Eva! Who—"

"She doesn't know," Jacinda announced.

"Ooh! Really?" The photographers surged forward. "Is that true, Eva? Give us a quote!"

"Jacinda's right. I don't know." Everyone shut up as soon as I opened my mouth. "It's sort of a secret."

"Another juicy secret!" Jacinda exclaimed, throwing an arm around my shoulders.

The flashbulbs exploded again, even more blinding and frantic than before.

"Marisela's mystery love child!"

"This story's gonna write itself!"

"Somebody better call the guys from Van Halen for a DNA test!"

"And Bon Jovi!"

"And Motley Crüe!"

"Our work here is done." Jacinda led me into the club, ignoring the photographers' pleas for just one more shot.

"Holy crap," I breathed.

"See how fun?"

"What have I done?" My throat went dry and my head started spinning. "What have I done?"

"You've just taken charge of your own life. Congratulations. This calls for a drink." She jerked me toward the bar, raising her voice as the DJ turned up the bass. "Here's your first red carpet lesson: never, ever let a photographer see you show weakness. If you can't think of a good answer to their question, smile enigmatically and count to three. Oh, and while I'm on the subject, don't let them see you eating, either, or smoking, drinking, picking a wedgie . . ."

She flashed a gratuitous display of cleavage at the bartender, who snapped to attention. "What can I get you?"

"I'll have a kir royale," she purred. "Thank you."

"I'll take two." I grabbed a frilly white cocktail napkin and dabbed the sweat off my forehead. "And a pack of cigarettes, if you have them."

Her eyes widened. "You really are freaked out, aren't you?"

"A little," I admitted, taking a big gulp of champagne.

"Well, slow down. I'm not going to spend my night baby-sitting a sloppy drunk."

Jacinda was telling *me* to slow down? Could the apocalypse be far behind?

"All the hot guys must be in the VIP section," she yelled. "Let's go check it out."

I tried to look enthusiastic.

"Don't be so morbid. You wanted your mom's attention, right? Well, this time, you'll definitely get it."

# 14

Danny finally called on Sunday afternoon. "Caleb said he called you yesterday. He claims the two of you are going to hang out again?" He sounded skeptical. "That you're officially dating now?"

"No. God, no," I assured him. "A thousand times no. C Money and I have had our one and only date for this lifetime."

"If only it were that simple."

"What do you mean?"

He sighed. "My dad makes everyone—me, Caleb, Nina, even my mom—have brunch together on Sunday mornings. It's this sick and twisted weekly ritual where we all pretend we like each other and we're this normal, healthy family."

"So?"

"So this morning, Nina picked me up at the dorm on the way to my mom's house—"

"Your mom really has brunch every week with her ex-husband and his new wife?"

"I told you, sick and twisted. Anyway, while we were in the car, I mentioned that I was planning to take you to the premiere on Wednesday. And Caleb just flipped out. Apparently, you're his boo." Danny started to laugh.

"This isn't funny! I am not his boo!"

"It's a little funny," he said. "He was waving his fists and threatening to cut me if I didn't 'step off his gambo.' He said, quote, You better get a whole stack of plates, homes, 'cause you about to get served.'"

I started laughing, too. "Shut up. He did not say that."

"And then he called me a flipperjabber."

"Well, he can call you whatever he wants," I said. "But I'm still not going out with him. I'm going out with you."

"Yeah, but Nina was driving the whole time this was going on. And he's her son. Her only child. Her main mission in life is to give him everything he wants, the instant he wants it. And since he wants you, I'm forbidden to date you."

*"Forbidden?* Are you kidding me?"

"That's the exact word she used: forbidden. Like it's the Eleventh Commandment: Thou shalt not date thy stepbrother's boo."

"For the last time, I'm not his boo!"

"So I told Nina that I'm nineteen years old, living on my own, and she can't forbid me to date anybody."

"What'd she say to that?"

"She said if I saw you again, she'd get my dad to stop paying my tuition. Which isn't even a good threat because most of my tuition is covered by my baseball scholarship."

"You play baseball?" I asked.

"Pitcher. Left-handed."

"Really? I love baseball. I'm a huge fan." Okay, so maybe I'd never actually sat down and *watched* a single inning, but it was high time I broadened my horizons. "When's your next game?"

He laughed again. "The season doesn't start till the end of February, superfan."

"February." I cleared my throat. "Right. I knew that."

"Anyway, then she said she can make my life miserable, scholarship or no scholarship, and yours, too. So until Caleb finds a new gambo to fixate on, we're officially—*dun, dun, duuunnn*—forbidden to see each other. Very Montague/Capulet."

Wait. Was this just an excuse to get out of our date on Wednesday? Was this a polite L.A. brush-off, à la "don't call us, we'll call you"?

"Oh. Okay." My blasé, sophisticated routine was getting better every day.

"But I told her that was never going to happen. I'm an adult, you're an adult, we can see each other if we want to."

"Yeah?" I perked up. "Nice. Fight the power."

There was a long pause. "That's when she called your aunt."

"She called Laurel? Today?"

"Around noon," he confirmed. "And she went off on a ten-minute rant. Then she finally stopped screaming, hung up, and told Caleb he had nothing to worry about because your aunt won't let you see me."

"She can't do that," I said, losing conviction with every syllable. My aunt hadn't clawed her way to the top of the Hollywood food chain by being a calm and fair-minded woman. Look who got me into this C Money mess in the first place. Who knew what else she was capable of?

I'd find out when she heard the news about my media debut at Troika last night. Gulp.

"According to Nina, your aunt said you're reserved for her little prince."

My jaw dropped. "The hell I am! She cannot 'reserve' me like a table at Ago. I'm not some mail-order bride or a prize goat that she can just, like, auction off at the county fair!"

"What? Who said you were a goat?"

"Nobody—not even Laurel Cordes—can make me date your stepbrother."

"True, but she *can* make your life hell. And so can Nina. It's her specialty. Trust me." His tone was rueful. "And if you ever want to get cast in a TV show . . ."

"Uh-uh. No way. I'm not going to whore myself out for a role in some crappy sitcom."

"Calm down a second. Here's what I'm thinking: we can't go to a premiere together, but what if we stay under the radar?"

"Low-profile dating?"

"Sure. If anyone asks, we can deny everything. Or say we're just friends."

"Ooh. That's so Brad and Angelina."

"It'll be fun. We can hang out and talk about your great love of baseball."

"I'm not going if you keep bringing that up," I warned.

"Friday night. We'll go to the Grove, hang out for a while, then maybe see a movie. Wait. I've got a better idea. How much do you know about poker?"

"Slightly less than I do about baseball."

"Doesn't matter, I can help you. There are a few bars out here that run tournaments every Friday."

"Bars? Gambling? And here I left my fake ID in Massachusetts."

"No problem. One of the few perks of being Nina's stepson—I have connections."

"Oh my God," Coelle said when she got back to the apartment on Sunday night. "I leave you two alone for forty-eight hours and this is what happens? You go to a club opening dressed like Christina Aguilera in the 'Dirrrty' video and start spreading rumors about *our agent's sister?*"

"Everything is totally under control," Jacinda insisted, sipping a smoothie and watching the latest episode of *My Super Sweet Sixteen*. "Look at that dress. How tragic. She should've spent a little less on sequins and a little more on her stylist."

"Fine. Ignore me," Coelle snitted. "When Laurel rips up your contract and changes the locks to this place, don't come bitching to me."

I furrowed my brow. "Do you really think she'll throw us out?"

Jacinda took another long, leisurely sip of her smoothie. "Nobody's going anywhere. Laurel's not about to let her most fabulous client slip through her fingers."

"But what about me?" I pressed.

"You're blood kin. You're safe."

Unless she found out about me and Danny.

Jacinda muted the TV for a commercial. "Besides, why would Laurel get mad? Your mom is the one who'll be upset, and you don't care about that. Serves her right for what she did to you."

Coelle turned to me, her dismay overruled by a hunger for fresh gossip. "What'd she do to you?"

"I don't want to get into it right now." I shook my head. "How'd the tampon commercial go?"

"How do you think it went?"

She sighed. "I'm the new face of fresh-scented feminine hygiene. Just what Cornell University is looking for."

"So when you have to go to New York for a shoot, where do you stay? Does the agency put you up in a hotel?"

"I wish. I have to stay with my parents."

"They live in a very swanky co-op overlooking Central Park," Jacinda interjected. "Coelle's daddy is the head of cardiology at the fanciest hospital in Manhattan."

"Yeah. He wants me to be a doctor, like him. Well, actually, what he really wanted was for me to be a boy. But when I wasn't, and he and my mom didn't have any more children, he decided that the next best thing was for me to be a surgeon. He's still hoping that the vet thing is just a phase. So is my mom. That's the one thing they agree on." She brightened. "Oh, that reminds me! I signed up to volunteer at the Humane Society and I told them you guys might come, too. We start next Tuesday."

"Can't," Jacinda said blithely. "Allergic to cats."

"You are not. You just don't want to deal with flea dips and dog poo."

"You got that straight," she agreed. "But have fun. I'm sure it'll look great on your college applications."

"Yeah. Maybe it'll make up for my horrible verbal SAT score. I have to skip my prep course next weekend to do press for *Twilight's Tempest*'s one thousandth episode party and the weekend after that to shoot that shaving gel commercial."

"Shaving gel, tampons . . . you're very well-groomed, aren't you?" I teased.

"I try." She shoved the sofa cushions aside and sat down next to us. "You coming to A and M class tomorrow?"

That would mean C Money, Smith the Sadist, and Bissy Billington all in one room. "Actually, I think I may be coming down with, uh, scurvy. Or rickets. Something."

Coelle narrowed her eyes. "You don't look sick to me."

I forced out a feeble cough.

"Oh, give it up, Eva." Jacinda laughed.

"I really do feel sick."

"If you feel sick now, how are you going to do when the press coverage about your mom starts up?" she asked.

"I'm planning on keeling over and dying."

"Go ahead and die, then, but be quiet about it because I'm

exhausted." Jacinda clicked off the television, treated us to a very unconvincing yawn, and trudged toward the stairs with sudden weariness.

Coelle smirked. "She's waiting for us to go to sleep, then she's sneaking out to party with her new mystery man. I've seen this routine a million times."

"Well, I don't think she'll be sneaking past me anytime soon." I gnawed my lower lip. "I couldn't fall asleep right now if you shot me up with a horse tranquilizer."

Coelle grabbed the purple chenille throw on the back of the sofa and wrapped it around her shoulders. "You're stressed about what happened with your mom?"

I nodded.

"Jacinda has a way of making a bad situation even worse. I'm going to bed, but if you're planning to stay up all night watching bad TV, I have some Godiva in my cupboard. Help yourself."

My eyebrows shot up. *"You* eat Godiva?"

"It was a gift," she said defensively. "I also have organic brussel sprouts, but I didn't think you'd be interested."

After an *Entourage* marathon on HBO, I raided the freezer for my leftover Cold Stone Creamery, but the ice cream container was missing. Jacinda's work, no doubt.

Around four o'clock, I must have dozed off in the middle of a TiVoed episode of *Lost,* because the next thing I knew, the phone was ringing, waking me up.

I lifted my head and glanced at the luminous numbers on the micowave clock: 6:45 A.M. Ugh. Jacinda's doing again: she kept forgetting to turn on her cell, so her stupid boyfriend was constantly calling on the landline at the weirdest times and then not saying a word if Coelle or I answered. He'd just hang up after a little heavy breathing (sicko). Well, two could play at that game. I picked up the receiver and slammed it down, then turned off the ringer, pulled the blanket over my head, and went back to sleep.

A few hours later, another kind of insistent ringing woke me up: the doorbell.

# 15

Harper looked positively ecstatic when I opened the door. Never a good sign.

"Well, well, well." Her lips curled up in a tight sneer as I rubbed my eyes and blinked in the bright morning sunlight. "If it isn't the illustrious Miss Cordes."

"Time is it?" I mumbled.

"Time to wake up and smell the coffee."

"Are you here for a reason? Or did you just miss me?"

"Here." She thrust a shiny silver flip phone at me. "Your aunt wanted me to give this to you. It's your new cellphone."

I stared down at the phone. "Oh. Thanks. But isn't it kinda early for—"

"Yes, actually, it *is* pretty damn early. But Laurel insisted that I buy this and bring it over the second the stores opened. I had to get up while it was still dark outside."

"What a shame," I said, sweet as pie. "I am *so* sorry about that."

"I even got you a three-one-oh area code. Most of West Hollywood is three-two-three or two-one-three these days, but Laurel demanded I get you the crème de la crème."

"Three-one-zero? Three-two-three? What's the difference?"

"Ask one of your little friends." Her voice oozed condescension. "They'll explain."

"But . . . you drove all the way out here at the crack of dawn to give me a cellphone? I don't get it."

At that exact instant, the phone started to ring.

"Better answer that." She walked away without a single glance back, probably because she was too busy rubbing her hands together, going *mwahahahahaaa.*

The phone kept ringing, despite my concerted efforts to ignore it. So I punched the talk button and braced myself for the worst. "Hello?"

"Eva Dominique Cordes."

My mouth went dry. "Hi, Aunt Laurel. I mean, Laurel. Just Laurel. Sorry."

"What the hell do you think you're doing?" Her voice was sharp as serrated steel. "I tried to call you a million times this morning and you *hung up on me!* You do not hang up on me. Ever! Got that?"

"Got it," I assured her. "Why were you trying to call me?"

I could hear her heels clicking on the marble floor of her

foyer. She must be pacing back and forth. "Don't play dumb with me."

"I'm not playing," I said meekly.

"Have you seen today's issue of *South of Sunset*?"

*Shit.* "No."

"Well, why don't you go look it over. And then call me back. You have twenty minutes. The clock starts now. And don't you dare blow me off again; you have a cellphone now."

Whoa. "Okay, I'll—"

Suddenly, my aunt's furious ranting faded away and a new, wavery voice came on the line. "How could you?"

"Mom?"

"I mean it, Eva! How could you do this to me? Do you have any idea how long I was in labor with you?" She stopped to blow her nose. *"Forty-eight hours. I practically died. I told the doctor that if it came down to a choice, he should save you instead of me."*

Last time I heard this story, it'd been thirty-six hours.

"Why don't you just come over and cut my heart out with a caviar knife?"

"Why don't *you* come over and cut *mine* out with a Harry Winston brooch?" I countered.

"You don't love me!" she wailed. "You've never loved me!"

"You don't deserve my love!" I raged. "What have you ever done for me since they cut the umbilical cord?"

Laurel piped up in the background. "Girls! Both of you! Stop it!"

"You are so ungrateful," my mother hissed. "You'll never know what I went through—"

"You're such a coward!" I retorted. "Why don't you just tell me who my father is? Give me a name and I'll never bother you again. Maybe *he'll* want to see how I turned out, even if you don't."

"Your father? Ha! Let me tell you something about your sainted daddy, you little—"

"Marisela! That is enough!" A series of muffled thumps followed. Obviously, Laurel was trying to wrestle the receiver back from Mom. "You're done using the phone until you can behave like a rational adult."

*"I am a rational adult!"* Mom shrieked so loudly that I had to hold the phone six inches away from my ear.

"Have another mimosa and go back to bed," my aunt directed, sounding tired. "Eva? You still there?"

I folded my arms, burning with resentment. "Yes."

"Listen. Your mom's a little . . . overwrought today. The lecture I planned to give you was just completely upstaged, but you get the picture: we are not happy over here."

Yeah. Like it was all rainbows and gumdrops over here. "I'll read the paper and call you back."

"Don't bother. I think your mom's said enough for everybody this morning. We'll all have a cooling-off period and then meet for dinner tonight."

"Ago?" I suggested. They wouldn't be able to murder me in a public place.

"My house," she said wryly, like she'd read my mind. "Your mother is too humiliated to show her face in public. Go to A and M class and try to stay out of trouble for the next twelve hours."

"But I hate—"

"Are you actually going to argue with me about this?

After what you pulled this weekend?" She sounded incredulous.

"No," I murmured.

"Good. And *be nice* to Caleb Marx. Nina said your behavior on Saturday night left a lot to be desired."

"That is such a lie! All I did was sit there the whole night and watch him—"

"Hey. What did I just say?" She started grinding her teeth. I could hear it over the phone. "Stay the hell away from his stepbrother and *keep your mouth shut*. I'll see you tonight."

•    •    •

Over-the-hill megamodel Marisela Cordes has a few skeletons in her closet alongside all the knockoff Hermès—turns out the former catwalker, who recently moved back to L.A. with a youthful new face and a youthful new man, has a not-so-youthful daughter, Eva. "I'm going to be the next big thing," the modest 18-year-old mademoiselle informed us at the opening of Troika last Saturday night. "I'm practically Hollywood royalty." Obviously she takes after her mother in the ego department . . . but who's the proud papa? "It's sort of a secret," laughed the little tease. Like mother, like daughter! Nobody's talking yet, but several stale pop stars are sweating visibly. The G-Spot gumshoes are on the case . . . stay tuned!

"My stars." Bissy finished scanning the newsprint in the front seat of Mrs. Billington's station wagon. "Did you really say all that?"

"No, I did not, Jacinda did." I had skipped breakfast—my Honey Nut Cheerios were inexplicably missing and I didn't have time to run out for a smoothie. Figuring that Jacinda had helped herself to my cereal, I retaliated by stealing three cans of her Red Bull, one of which I had chugged before meeting up with Bissy and her mom. Coelle had left at 5:00 A.M. to film her infamous swimsuit scene, so I was going to be stuck at A and M class with just Bissy and C Money. And caffeine. Lots and lots of caffeine.

"Well, you sound like a spoiled, stuck-up diva," Bissy said. "Who hates her parents."

Mrs. Billington tsk-tsked. "Someone needs to work on her interview skills."

"But I didn't *say* anything!" I repeated. "I just stood there, paralyzed with panic, and Jacinda started spouting all this crap about 'It' girls and Hollywood dynasties."

"Well, that's the first rule of interviews right there, mini-muffin: never let someone else do all the talkin'." Mrs. Billington fluffed her fried, dyed, and pushed-to-the-side hair. "Young ladies today are so inarticulate. Now, if you had grown up doing pageants like my Bissy, you wouldn't have lost your composure."

Bissy turned around to give me an angelic smile.

"So . . ." Mrs. Billington tapped her perfect pink nails on the steering wheel. "Who *is* your dad, honey bun?"

"I don't know," I mumbled.

"Oh, you can tell me." She dropped her voice to a whisper. "It'll be our little secret."

"I don't *know,*" I repeated, getting more exasperated by the second.

"But in that article, it says—"

"The article's wrong."

Mrs. Billington got all miffed. "Where I come from, well-bred young ladies would never take that tone with their elders. But I suppose that's what comes of being raised by an international party girl and no father figure."

Things went from bad to worse at A & M class. Word had already spread about the G-Spot, and general consensus was that I was an insufferable drama queen who was so self-centered I had my own gravitational field. No one would say a word to me.

No one, that is, except C Money.

"Boo," he whispered as we stretched out on our warm-up mats. "Hey, boo. I saw you in the paper today."

I ignored him.

"That interview was hot. You're supa fine and you know it. Ain't nothing wrong with that!"

I whipped my head back. "I didn't say any of that stuff! The reporters misquoted me!"

"Taken out of context?" He chortled. "You can't fool me with that worn-out line. But it's cool—I like my women feisty. When we gonna crisp again? We both know we had a connection on Saturday."

"No, you had a connection with your sake."

"How's Friday?"

"I'm busy." With Danny.

"A supa fine woman like yourself needs a supa fine man by her side. Why are you denyin' yourself?"

"Guess I just like punishment."

"Yeah? What else you like, *mami?*"

I tried to phrase this in his mother tongue so he would understand: "Step off, homes."

Before he could respond, Smith strode through the door, clapping his hands and yelling, "All right, people, today we're going to get in touch with our inner *animus*. I'm going to assign each of you a wild animal, and you must stay in character for the rest of the day."

Bissy squealed with delight upon being chosen as a butterfly. Caleb was named a noble stag, and immediately commenced charging across the room, hands splayed in front of his head like antlers.

Me? I had to be a bear.

"A bear?" I repeated, hoping there'd been some kind of misunderstanding.

"Correct." Smith nodded.

"But what kind of bear? A polar bear? A grizzly bear? A teddy bear?"

"Bears don't talk," Smith snapped.

Fine. If he was leaving the choice up to me, I'd be a hibernating bear. I lumbered over to the corner, careful to avoid the galloping stag, neighing horse, and wildly caroming butterfly, curled up, and tried to fall asleep.

*Thwack!* A hard, heavy object hit me right above the kidneys.

"Ow!" I rocketed up into a sitting position.

"Bears don't talk!" Smith crowed, lobbing another full Evian bottle at me.

I successfully dodged his water-filled missile, rubbing my back. "What the—"

At this point, he uncapped one of the remaining bottles and started splashing water on me. "Wake up, Mama Bear! Spring is here!"

Laurel was actually paying him for this? "This is so not cool." I ducked back into my corner.

"I can't heeear you!"

"Grr!" I rolled my eyes and bared my teeth. "Roar!"

"Are you reacting as a bear or a person?" he feigned confusion. "I can't tell!"

I contemplated mauling him and leaving the mangled corpse for the park rangers, but I knew my aunt couldn't handle even one more phone call about my insubordination. So I extended one mighty paw and swiped menacingly at the air in front of me. "Growr!"

"Ooh, the bear is angry!" Smith traded in his water bottle for a ballpoint pen. "She must be protecting her cubs! What will she do when a wayward hiker pokes her with a stick?"

We never found out because the stag (who apparently needed to take his shirt off to feel truly deerlike) lowered his antlers and charged my tormentor, slipping on a puddle of water and crashing into Smith, who went flying into the mirrored wall.

"Ooh." I flinched as the mirror cracked on contact with Smith's skull. "That's gonna leave a mark."

Sure enough, when he reeled back from the wall, a large red bump was already swelling up on his forehead.

"Careful!" Bissy and I cried in unison as he stepped on another slippery patch of floor.

Too late. Flailing and cursing, Smith collapsed.

Everybody stopped braying and mooing and meowing to watch the fallout. We held our collective breath as Smith grabbed the barre running along the wall, hauled himself to his feet, and grabbed his tailbone.

"Class dismissed," was all he said.

We skittered out the door in silence, leaving our animal selves behind (except for Bissy, who continued sashaying on tiptoe and fluttering her arms).

"I'm your hero," Caleb informed me as we loitered in the lobby, waiting for Mrs. Billington to pick us up. "Your knight in shining bling."

"If you say so." I cracked open my second Red Bull, hoping the sugar would give me the strength to get through this conversation.

"So show me proper 'preciation. When we going to go get crunk again?"

"Caleb, listen—"

His face turned crimson. "Don't ever call me Caleb! My name is C Money, hear? *C Money!*"

"Whoa." I backed up a few steps. "Okay . . . C. Listen, I'm glad you had a good time on Saturday, but I'm not sure that we're, you know, meant to be."

"Oh, we're meant to be. Don't even doubt it. We're, like, all destined and star-crossed and shit. Like . . ." His eyes glazed over as he tried to think of an appropriate example. "He-Man and Teela."

Bissy bounced into the middle of our conversation, her blond ponytail bobbing. "We have to go, Eva. Momma's parked outside and it's rude to keep her waiting."

"Oh, darn." I tried to look crestfallen as I waved good-bye to C. "Gotta go."

"We'll kick it this weekend." He flashed me his trademark white-boy gang sign.

"He is so vile," Bissy sniffed as she walked out to the parking lot. "Why do you even talk to him? Are you *that* desperate for a boyfriend?"

"His mother is Nina Marx," I responded in the same passive-aggressive simper. "The casting director. Didn't you know?"

"Really?" Her eyes widened. "And he's single? Maybe I should give him my number."

"Maybe you should." Now *she* would be the perfect Teela to his He-Man.

When we got into the Volvo (today's migraine-inducing musical selection: Neil Diamond), Mrs. Billington announced, "We have to take a quick detour to Century City. Bissy's got a callback for a national commercial. You don't mind, do you, cookie?"

"Anything for Bissy," I said, my heart racing from sugar shock.

Mrs. Billington yammered on about her daughter's star potential until we reached a small, nondescript brick building on a quiet street. We piled out of the car and opened the front door, which led to a small waiting area. Bissy signed in on a clipboard while I took a seat in one of the flimsy metal folding chairs and started jiggling my foot.

About ten other thin, blond teenage girls were milling

around, practicing their lines and trying to psych each other out.

"I'm coming off my third national commercial in under a month—let's hope the fourth time's a charm!"

"Good luck. This director is great to work with. I've done two other projects with her and she's amazing."

"Really? I haven't worked with her yet, but, you know, once you've done a screen test for Scorsese like I have, you can work with just about anyone."

A couple of girls tried to draw me into their web of intimidation, but I shook my head and pointed to Bissy. "I'm not auditioning, just along for the ride."

"Then why do you look so hyper?" one of the blonde-bots demanded.

"Chemical stimulants," I replied.

"Oh. Okay then." She wandered off to inflict her story about her close, personal friendship with Jessica Alba on someone else.

The bragging and posturing and reciting of lines ceased the moment a door opened to reveal a schlumpy, denim-clad man who looked like he hadn't slept in weeks.

"All right, girls." He grabbed the sign-in clipboard and scanned the list of names. "You're all here for the Samba callback? We'll see you in the order you arrived. Please make sure you've got your head shots ready and your cellphones turned off before you go in to see the director. Let's make this as quick as possible."

Oh boy. Any time a man holding a clipboard says "Let's make this as quick as possible," you *know* it's gonna take all damn day. And of course we'd been last to arrive, so Bissy would be last to read.

I was so bored I started in on my third Red Bull, after which I found myself physically incapable of sitting still.

"Eva, sugarplum, you're makin' me nervous," Mrs. Billington said. "Would you please simmer down?"

"Can't. Sorry."

Finally it was Bissy's turn. After five minutes in the Room o' Judgment, she stumbled back into the waiting room, looking pale and confused.

"What's wrong?" Mrs. Billington leapt to her feet and shook her daughter's shoulders. "What happened in there?"

"They . . . they wanted me to dance," Bissy said weakly.

"Well, that's good, right? All that time and money we spent on tap and ballet lessons is finally gonna pay off!"

Bissy started toward the exit, sounding close to tears. "But they didn't want tap or ballet, Momma, they wanted—"

"Hey!" Clipboard Man called out behind us. "Where are you going?"

We turned around. "M-me?" Bissy quavered.

"No." He pointed straight at me. "You."

# 16

After glancing over my shoulder to make sure he was really and truly pointing at me, I turned back to the clipboard guy and said, "Oh, I'm not auditioning."

He tapped his clipboard. "Are you an actress?"

"Well, yeah."

"No, she's not!" Bissy couldn't contain herself. "She just got here last week!"

He ignored her. "Do you have an agent?"

I nodded. "Laurel Cordes."

"Why don't you come in and read for us?" He raked a hand through his bushy brown hair. "I'm Steve, I'm the casting director, and I'm desperate to find someone for this commercial. What's your name?"

"Eva Cordes."

"Eva." He scribbled this down. "Please, come on in."

"She's hasn't prepared!" Mrs. Billington protested. "She doesn't even have a head shot!"

Steve waved this away. "We'll do a Polaroid for today—no big deal."

"She doesn't have SAG membership!" Bissy yelled.

Steve frowned at the mother-daughter team from hell. "If she's not SAG, we'll work it out. Calm down, ladies."

*"This is a mistake!"* Mrs. Billington elbowed me aside. "My Bissy is the one you want!"

I headed toward the side door. "I'm ready."

Steve ushered me into a large room equipped with bright lights, a large camera, and several masking tape Xs on the floor. Four very cranky-looking women in business suits sat behind a conference table, shuffling through head shots.

"All right, ladies, last one," Steve announced. "This is Eva." He introduced me to the assembled suits: "This is Kelly, the director; Nora, who represents our client, Samba Sunless Tanner; and Heather and Zoe, who work for the ad agency."

I heard a door slam out in the waiting room. There went my ride home. Oh well.

"So Eva." Kelly, a wiry redhead, was obviously down to her last nerve. "You don't have a head shot?"

"I have one, but not with me."

"Do you have any professional dance experience?"

"Not exactly. I just moved to L.A., and I wasn't planning to start auditioning quite yet—"

"Let me cut to the chase. Our client—" she nodded at Nora—"is a high-end line of skin care products looking to move into the teen market. We want fun, we want flirty, we want offbeat."

"And we *don't* want just another blond beach bunny," Nora added.

"Right. We need a girl who can be both elegant and playful, who embodies the spontaneous spirit of Samba sunless tanner. Here's our vision." Kelly put both hands up in an L shape to frame an imaginary camera angle. "You're an average teenage girl stuck inside during a long, cold winter. You're daydreaming about spring break, when you'll be frolicking on the beach with your hunky boyfriend. And do you want to be white and pasty when spring break comes along?" She looked at me expectantly.

"No?" I guessed.

"Right." She grinned like I'd just aced quantum mechanics. "You want to look sun-kissed and toned. So for this commercial, you'll pretend to be dancing around your bedroom, lip-synching into a hairbrush and imagining how hot you'll look when summer rolls around."

Wait. Hadn't I already seen this clip? Like, in every single cheesy teen movie ever made?

"What?" Nora asked when she saw my face.

"Nothing." I tried to look enthusiastic. "Sounds great."

"No, really," she persisted. "I'm always interested in feedback from our target market. What's wrong?"

I shrugged. "Well, nothing's *wrong*, exactly, but isn't the whole dancing around with a hairbrush thing a little clichéd?"

As soon as I said it, I knew I'd made a huge mistake. Steve cringed, Kelly gasped, the ad agency reps looked ready to call in a hit man.

But Nora nodded thoughtfully. "You've seen it before?"

"Every time I turn on the TV."

"So we might need to scrap the whole idea . . ."

"We can't." Heather flattened her palm on the table. "We have to start production this weekend if we want to air for the Super Bowl. And you already paid for the airtime."

But Nora wasn't finished. ". . . *or* we could add a new twist."

"Like what?" Heather asked.

"Like what?" Kelly asked.

"Like what?" Zoe asked.

"I'm not sure." Nora smiled. "Surprise us." She gestured to a small stereo in the corner. "Show us something we *don't* see every time you turn on TV."

All I can say is that the Red Bull took over from there. I pushed PLAY on the stereo, and as the music started (an upbeat, highly danceable Gorillaz groove), Nora called, "Come on, Eva! Wow us with moves we've never seen before!"

So I did. I jammed, I grooved, I dropped it like it was hot. And that was just the beginning. I leaned back, two-stepped, pop-locked, showed off a milkshake that would bring all the boys to the yard, and threw in a little Vogueing and what I was pretty sure was the Macarena for good measure.

By the time I finished, I was seeing spots and my heart felt like it was going to explode. "Thank you and good night," I panted, stepping back to gauge the reaction of my audience. "Don't forget to tip your waitress."

Heather and Zoe could not have looked more horrified if I had just spit in their coffee.

Kelly had grabbed a pack of cigarettes and lit up, despite the NO SMOKING sign displayed prominently next to the doorway, and puffed away with an air of grim foreboding.

But Nora was laughing so hard tears streamed down her cheeks. So hard she could barely speak. "Oh my God." She turned to the cameraman. "Tell me you got that."

"It's always a good sign when the client laughs," Steve whispered as he ushered me out. "Expect a call this afternoon."


"You didn't tell me you were a dancer." When Laurel called my brand-new cell for the second time in twelve hours, she was in a much better mood.

I dumped a cup of detergent into the washing machine in the apartment complex's laundry room. "You heard about the audition?"

"Not only did I hear about it, I talked money, honey! You got it! You're the new Samba Sunless Tanning girl."

"Shut up! Are you kidding me?"

"I never kid when residuals are involved, pet. And you're going to get a lot of them. This ad's going to debut during the Super Bowl. Do you know what that means?"

"The entire country's going to see me shake my booty in boy shorts and a tank top?" Once the Red Bull finally wore off, I'd started feeling a little mortified about all this.

"The entire *world*," she corrected. "Easiest money either of us will ever make. They loved you. Said you had great skin tone, great legs, great attitude."

"Somebody actually said I have a great attitude?" That was a first.

"Yes they did, and there's no reason for them to ever find out the truth. And they loved that you're not blond and buxom."

Another first.

"So pet, all champagne and confetti aside, what happened in there today? I thought this was Bissy's audition?"

"It was, but I didn't do anything wrong, swear to God. Mrs. Billington dragged me over after A and M class. I was just hanging out in the waiting room and they asked me to come in and audition."

"You've got that vulnerability," she breathed. I could practically hear the cash register ringing between her ears. "That charisma. Just like your mother."

"Speaking of which." I turned on the washing machine and headed back to the apartment. "Does this mean all is forgiven?"

"I forgive you as long as you come in and sign contracts tomorrow. Marisela is another story."

My whole body stiffened at the mere mention of her name. "I don't care if *she* forgives me or not."

"Yes, you do."

"No, I don't. I really don't."

"Then it's gonna be a tense family dinner tonight."

I rolled my eyes. "I still have to come?"

"Yes, you do. Seven sharp. And can I give you a piece of aunty advice?"

"If you must."

"Don't wear yellow for the Samba shoot."

"Good luck in there, soldier." Jacinda pulled her convertible up to the elaborate gates blocking my aunt's driveway, rolled down the window, and buzzed the intercom. "No matter what they threaten you with, don't give them anything but your name, rank, and serial number."

"Whatever. I'm not worried," I blustered. "What can she do to me that's worse than what she'd already done? And anyway, who needs a mother when I've got my name in the paper and a national commercial? Pretty soon she'll be *begging* me to be seen with her, but I won't even take her calls."

Jacinda nodded. "Revenge is a dish best served with a heaping side order of fame and fortune."

"So true. Thanks for the ride, by the way."

"No problem." She slammed the car into drive as the gates swung open. "I have places to go and people to see, and this happens to be on my way."

I arched one eyebrow. "Another rendezvous with Anonyman?"

"I cannot confirm or deny that," she said in her best press conference voice.

"Well, just don't call me from a Mexican prison at three A.M. Or a Vegas wedding chapel, all drunk and legally married."

"Please. There's not enough alcohol on the Strip to make me forget to sign a prenup."

"Famous last words." I gave her my most trustworthy look. "Come on, Jacinda, who is he?"

"Nobody."

"Come on, give me a hint. Just his first name. I won't tell anyone!"

"No way. Too much of your life ends up in the G-Spot."

I tried a new tack. "Why so secretive? Is it really that sordid? Is he older?"

She flushed.

"With a checkered past?"

Her flush got redder.

*"Married?"*

She finally cracked. "Of course not!"

"But he *is* older with a checkered past?" I pressed.

"It's none of your business." She reached across me, shoved open the passenger side door, and pointed imperiously at the limestone steps to the house. "Out."

"Fine." I got out of the car and shut the door. She peeled out, leaving faint skidmarks on the inlaid brick and nearly running over my left foot. I watched the silver convertible glint in the sun as she raced away, then trudged up the steps to face the fallout from my first red carpet appearance.

"You have ruined my life." My mother wiped her eyes with the back of her hand, smudging mascara all over her cheek. Just like the last time I'd seen her. You'd think she'd invest in some waterproof Maybelline. "I've done nothing but love you and you've made my life hell. Why do you hate me? Is it because I didn't breast-feed you?"

"Marisela." Aunt Laurel put down her fork and frowned at my mom across the black oval wenge wood dining table. "I thought we agreed we were finished with the histrionics."

Mom pouted into her salad. She looked a little tired and pale, but her shiny black hair was ready for a close-up, as usual. "I'm trying to hold it together, but I just . . . I can't cope." She bunched up her starched linen napkin. "I'm a so-cial leper."

I chewed a huge bite of risotto and mumbled something that I hoped she might take as an apology. Because if she was waiting for me to throw myself at her feet and actually say the word "sorry," she'd be waiting until that diamond necklace turned to dust.

"You wanted to act out? You wanted to humiliate me?" She snatched up the copy of *South of Sunset* that she had hidden in her lap and waved it under my nose. "Well, mission accomplished! I hope it was worth it."

"Isn't one of you supposed to be the *parent?*" Aunt Laurel asked pointedly.

Between all the fine china, the hand-painted blue silk wallpaper, and the massive chandelier dripping in crystal, Laurel's dining room could have been used as a set for *Masterpiece Theatre*.

But the mood tonight was definitely more *Surreal Life*.

"Solutions, Mari." My aunt reached down to pat Rhett, who was racing around the table, begging for scraps and nipping at our ankles. "We're focusing on solutions. There's no point in browbeating Evie anymore."

"Yes, there is," Mom insisted. "I want her to apologize. And mean it."

"Well, I want *you* to admit you have a child," I retorted. "We all want things, I guess."

Her beautiful face took on a very bizarre expression of murderous-but-Botoxed fury. "Don't you talk to me that way! Your grandparents raised you better than that."

"How would you know?" I asked, all light and casual. "All your calls and visits?"

"Knock it off, both of you! We need to stick together and work on damage control." Laurel ran her dinner table just like she'd run her agency meetings—with an iron fist in a Gucci glove. "First and foremost, we *all* have to stop leaking information about your father. If we all say 'no comment' enough times, the press will get bored and go away. There'll be a few more days of scrutiny and then this whole thing will blow over."

"What if it doesn't?" my mother asked. "What if they just keep hounding us?"

"They won't," Laurel declared. "No offense, Mari, but you're not the A-lister you once were."

Mom choked on her lettuce.

"But we have to be united in silence. Eva, I'm looking at you."

"Don't worry about me." I shot a look at my mother. "I *can't* tell them anything else—I don't even know who he is."

"That's right, and now you know why I didn't tell you," she retorted. "You can't keep a secret."

"But you sure can. None of your boyfriends know who I am, nobody in the entire world knows who my dad is . . ." I stopped midsentence when I saw it—the Look. My mother glanced at Aunt Laurel, and Aunt Laurel glanced back. The whole exchange flashed by in under a second, but I knew.

"Wait." I rounded on my aunt. "You know who my dad is, don't you?"

She broke eye contact and ducked down to feed Rhett a bite of risotto off her spoon.

I gasped. "You know! You've known all this time!"

"Don't be ridiculous," Mom said, smoothing out her napkin. "Of course she doesn't know."

"Then what was that look about?" I demanded.

"What look?" my mother scoffed. "There was no look."

Ha. I knew a Look when I saw one and that? Was a Look.

My aunt stopped fussing with the poodle and sat up straight. "I honestly don't know who your dad is, pet. Promise."

"Where have I heard that line before?" I mused, crinkling up my forehead. "Oh, I know: when you lied to me about not knowing where Mom was!"

She raised her right hand like she was about to recite the Pledge of Allegiance. "If there was anything to tell, I'd tell you, I swear, but I don't know."

She stared me down over a crystal bowl of freshly cut tulips.

I stared right back.

Mom dropped her wineglass on the table with a clatter and grabbed my napkin to soak up the spreading stain. "Oops. So! Everybody ready for dessert?"

"I'm going to the bathroom." I pushed back my chair and headed for the hallway, narrowly escaping one of Rhett's razor-toothed ambushes from under the table.

As I retreated down the hall, the voices in the dining room dropped to urgent whispers.

I slipped out of my shoes and crept back toward the dining room, keeping my breaths silent and shallow. When I reached the doorway, I flattened myself against the wall and listened with all my might.

"I can't believe you put me on the spot like that," Laurel was hissing. "Now when she finds out the truth, she's going to hate us both!"

"Well, what else could I do?" Mom hissed back. "You're the one who was throwing the meaningful looks around!"

"If I hear one more word about that alleged 'look' . . . Listen, Mari. She's not stupid. She knows something's up. You're going to have to tell her someday."

"I can't tell her!" Mom squawked. "You know that better than anyone! Can you imagine the fallout?"

Silence as my aunt pondered this.

"She's better off not knowing," Mom said. The firm confidence in her voice surprised me. She had stopped whining and taken charge. "She's so angry at me anyway, she might as well hate me for this, too. We'll all be better off. You still have the papers, right? In a secure location?"

"Yes, I told you, they're filed away safe and sound."

"Are you *sure?* Because if those ever get out—"

"I'm sure. Nobody suspects a thing."

I closed my eyes and tried to pick up any sound, any movement from around the corner, but in my frustrated attempt to hear more, I banged my forehead against the doorframe.

Rhett went wild, barking and snarling like a bloodthirsty Doberman.

"What's wrong, baby?" Laurel trilled. "Do you hear something?"

My heart thudding like the subwoofer in C Money's Hummer, I raced down the hall, scooped up my shoes, darted into the bathroom, and closed the door behind me as quietly as possible. After a few minutes of sweaty-palmed trembling, I splashed my face with cold water and headed out.

On the way back to the dining room, I passed the door to my aunt's study. The room where, presumably, she stored all her important papers and files.

From: OutOfEden@globecon.com <eva cordes>
To: descartesismybizatch@wordup.net <Jeff Oerte>
Subject: S.O.S! CALL ME
Jeff—
You can't STILL be mad at me. And even if you are, I need
you to forgive me for half an hour. Okay?
I really need someone to talk to.
Please call me.
310-555-2384
Operators are standing by.
Hopefully,
Eva

# 17

"Papers? What kind of papers?" Jacinda demanded the next afternoon as we picked at our skinless chicken and grilled veggies at Koo Koo Roo, L.A.'s "healthy" fast-food chain.

"I have no clue. This is the first I've heard about any of this. Laurel said she's keeping all these important papers in a secure location. And it has something to do with my father." I passed a plastic knife to Coelle, who used it to trim any remaining fat molecules off her chicken breast.

"You think she's known who he is all this time?" Jacinda asked.

"It sure sounded like it from the conversation I over-heard."

"Eavesdropping?" Coelle rolled her eyes. "How mature."

I shrugged. "Hey, a girl's gotta do what a girl's gotta do."

Jacinda made a face as Coelle methodically dissected everything on her plate. "Are you going to eat any of that, or just stab it? You know it's already dead, right?"

Coelle ignored her and kept talking to me. "Maybe you should start eavesdropping on Jacinda. Get to the bottom of her little, you know, tryst. Rendezvous. Assignation."

"Ooh, three points to the walking thesaurus." I put down my cup and gave her a smattering of golf-clap applause.

"Thank you. I'm starting the SAT prep course. Again. Later this week, I'll be busting out 'craven,' 'indefatigable,' and 'disenfranchised.'"

"I can hardly wait."

"Yawn." Jacinda gave up on her fat-free dinner and grabbed a mirror out of her purse to begin her customary post-meal lip gloss application. "Why do you keep torturing yourself with that stupid test?"

Coelle looked exasperated. "Don't you know *anything* about the college admissions process?"

"No. I have no use for higher education." Jacinda dabbed the pearly pink liquid onto her lower lip. "I'm planning on being a heartbreakingly beautiful young burnout, like Marilyn Monroe or Jean Harlow."

I choked down a big bite of broccoli. "So you would prefer *death* to reading a few textbooks?"

"Look at me." She threw out her arms in a dramatic flourish. "I'm made for the *world*, not the classroom."

Coelle snorted. "The peroxide has finally soaked through to her brain."

"By the way, how was your big date last night?" I asked.

"You didn't get any calls from the Mexican authorities, did you?" She shifted her weight and adjusted the strap of her shoe. "Enough about me. What about you, Ms. Early Graduation? Are you planning to go to college?"

"Of course," I said automatically.

"Then what the hell are you doing out here?" Jacinda finished up on her lips and started scrutinizing her manicure. "Shouldn't you be touring campuses and checking the mail eighteen times a day and giving yourself ulcers over whether you'll be waitlisted at Wellesley?"

"Well, the truth is, I already got accepted," I admitted. "Early decision at Leighton College. You probably haven't heard of it; it's a small liberal arts school in—"

"Alden, Massachusetts," Coelle finished for me. "Of course I've heard of it. It's right up there with Amherst and Williams."

"Yeah. Well, I was accepted in December, and since it was early decision I couldn't apply anywhere else. But, um . . ." I studied my vegetables like they might contain tomorrow's winning lottery numbers. "I don't think I'm going to go. There's this girl in my high school whose sole mission in life is to destroy me—"

"The infamous Brynn Kistler?" Jacinda asked.

"Yeah, Brynn Kistler," I confirmed. "Well, her father is the dean of the college. And her mother is dean of students. And a few things have happened since I applied."

"Like you had a higher calling to glamour and glory? Girl, I am right there with you." Jacinda nodded knowingly. "On the way home, can we please stop and get a chocolate shake? I'm dying over here."

"You're going to get fat if you keep eating fries and shakes instead of veggies," Coelle warned.

"I think you're dieting enough for both of us," Jacinda responded. "Relax, have a burger or two. The swimsuit scene's over, right?"

"Yeah, but I have a hot tub scene coming up next week."

"God. Are you working for a soap opera or the Playboy channel?"

As we gathered up our crumpled napkins and plastic plates, I thought about what Jacinda had said about having a higher calling to act. Maybe I was the same—I'd gotten a national commercial my first week here, hadn't I? Maybe I was a natural. Maybe this was what I was supposed to do with the rest of my life.

Or maybe I was just too scared and ashamed to go home and chase after the dreams I'd had before I made one bad decision that ruined everything.

"You know what I need?" Jacinda held the door as we filed out into the parking lot. "A new wardrobe. I'm bored to tears with every single outfit I own. They're all so bland and blah and—"

"All over our living room floor," Coelle interjected.

"Shut it, Martha. I'm going shopping. And since I'm driving, guess what? You guys are going shopping, too."

I shook my head. "I'm never going shopping with you again."

"Oh my God, would you get over that already?" She strutted toward her Mercedes, turning heads on both sides of the street. "It was a joke, babe. A joke!"

"Fine, then," I said loftily. "You won't mind if *I* pick out a few things for *you* this time."

Two hours later, Coelle and I were camped out on the floor of Neiman Marcus, waiting for Jacinda to decide among ten little black dresses.

"Do you think we could wrap this up sometime tonight?" Coelle tapped her pen against her folded copy of the *L.A. Times* (she was doing the crossword puzzle between arguments with Jacinda).

"Five more minutes," Jacinda promised. "I'm almost done."

"Just pick one," Coelle urged. "They're all black, short, and low cut, so what's the difference?"

Jacinda emerged from the dressing room wearing a black satin cocktail dress with chiffon zigzagging down the bodice. "Okay. This one is Zac Posen. Do you like this more or less than the Yigal Azrouel?"

I blinked. "Which one was that again?"

Coelle dropped her head into her hands. "They all look exactly the same."

"They do not!" She looked increasingly agitated with each new dress. I'd never seen her unsure of herself and I hoped I never would again. "The faster you give me some decent feedback, the faster we'll get out of here."

I rubbed my neck and tried to be patient. "Why don't you just pick your five favorites, put them on hold, think it over, and come back tomorrow?"

"Tomorrow? Are you high? I need a dress for tonight! Now pull your head out of your ass and *help me!*"

"What is going on with you?" Coelle gave her a long, hard look, then started nodding. "Oh, I get it. This is about a guy."

"What?" She stamped her foot. "It is not!"

"Oh, yes." Coelle put down the crossword puzzle and turned to me. "It's not going well with mystery man. She's trying to get his attention back by wearing a slutty dress."

"Ha! You couldn't be more wrong!" She unzipped the dress, let it fall in a puddle by her feet, stepped over it, and stomped back into the changing room. "Everything is going great. *He adores me!*"

She slammed the door so hard three saleswomen came running to make sure a wall hadn't collapsed.

One of us had to be decisive or we'd be here until the end of time. "Get the one with the halter top and the sequins," I called.

She stuck her head out. "The Alberta Ferretti?"

"Yeah." I had no idea if that was the correct designer, but I wanted my freedom back. "That was hot."

"Really?"

Coelle and I glanced at each other. "Definitely," she said. "White hot."

"The hottest thing you've tried on tonight, by far."

A few minutes later, she came out of the dressing room with the Alberta Ferretti in-hand and a dozen discarded options littering the floor. "See? That wasn't so hard."

"Right." Coelle filled in the final blanks in her crossword puzzle. "Now let's pay and go home."

Jacinda laughed, whipping out her wallet. "Home? *Mais non*. Honey, I still need to find shoes."

"So how are you going to find out about your dad?" Jacinda interrogated me while we tried on obscenely overpriced high heels.

"I'm not sure," I admitted, sticking out my right foot to admire a bejeweled gold lamé sandal. "I've Googled my mom and every guy I know she dated—"

"Screw that Encyclopedia Brown stuff. What you have to do is break into Laurel's house and ransack her study."

"Oh, okay." I rolled my eyes. "I can't believe I didn't think of that before."

"Me, either. It's totally obvious." She tossed some leopard-print mary janes back in their box and reached for a crystal-trimmed pump. "So when should we do it? Does she have any business trips coming up this month?"

"Jacinda. Be serious. I'm not breaking into my aunt's house."

She slipped on the pumps and took a few steps forward. "Sure you are. And we're going to help."

" 'We'? Who exactly is this 'we'?" Coelle piped up.

"The three of us." She held up her hand before Coelle could protest. "It'll be a bonding experience. Oprah would approve."

But I was on to her. "This is another one of your little schemes to screw me over. You just want that bathroom to yourself."

She tried to look wounded. "How can you say that? Besides, it's too late to get rid of you. You got a commercial, you're making money for Laurel, you're here to stay."

"Machiavellian, but true," Coelle agreed.

I tapped my fingernails against the armrest of the shoe department's cushy leather chair. "But even if we *did* manage to get into Laurel's study, how would we know what to look for?"

"Step one, pull papers out of filing cabinet," Jacinda explained, as if talking to a toddler. "Step two, read printing on paper. The old pull 'n read. Foolproof." She paused to ooh and ahh over a pair of patent leather slingbacks. "I'm trying these on."

"But the problem's going to be getting past the entry gate and the security system," I said. "Laurel always sets the alarm when no one's home; she's the paranoid type."

Jacinda sat back down and waved the slingbacks at the salesclerk. "If we need to get past the alarm, we'll just call in our trusty codebreaker."

"And that would be . . ."

She grinned. "Coelle."

Coelle crammed her feet into some feather-trimmed ballet flats. "Since when do I know anything about codebreaking?"

"You work on a TV series where there's a breaking and entering every other week. Take some notes next time. How hard could it be?"

I threw up my hands. "Let's go over the difference between TV and real life *one more time*—"

"You guys are making this way too complicated," Coelle said, finally resigning herself to the fact that she couldn't escape Jacinda's machinations. "We don't need to get all *Alias* with the alarm. We just have to figure out the code. Eva, next time you talk to your aunt, try to find out whatever you can about the big dates in her life. Birthdays, anniversaries, whatever. The alarm code's probably going to be a number that corresponds to one of those. Then make up an excuse to go home with her after work one night and try to see which keys she pushes to disarm the system."

"Check out the brainy chick in the flats," Jacinda marvelled.

"Yeah, well, if you're going to force me to participate in this, I'm going to make damn sure Laurel doesn't find out."

"Don't worry," Jacinda said. "I do this stuff all the time and I hardly ever get caught."

# 18

"Should I be wearing dark sunglasses and a fedora?" I asked when Danny picked me up for our stealth date on Friday. "Do we need to circle the block a few times to make sure we're not being followed?"

He laughed, touching my back to steer me toward his car. "No need—I'll drive way too fast for anyone to keep up." He opened the passenger side door to his vintage (and by "vintage," I mean ancient, dented, and rusted) gold Mercedes. "Have you been to the Grove yet?"

"No, but I hear it's quite the hot spot."

"It's basically a glorified outdoor mall—Crate and Barrel, the Gap, whatever—but behind the mall is the Farmer's Market, which is where you find the good stuff. Great coffee, great pizza, great tacky souvenirs."

I grinned. "Yeah, I was wondering how I'd survived this long without an I 'heart' Hollywood T-shirt."

"A T-shirt?" He ushered me into the passenger seat. "No, no. What you need are neon green sunglasses in the shape of palm trees and a salt shaker that looks like the Capitol Records building."

"Will we be picking up a map of the stars' homes after that?"

"If you're really lucky. You look great, by the way."

"Thanks." For a girl who was trying to stay under the radar, I'd put a whole lot of effort into wardrobe and makeup. Those new boots I'd bought at Neiman Marcus had come in handy today. I'd paired them with jeans, a feather-light blue cashmere sweater I'd borrowed from Coelle, and diamond-and-peridot earrings—which supposedly brought out my eyes—from Jacinda.

"So I got my first commercial," I announced as he turned the key in the ignition and the car shuddered to life. "We're filming this weekend."

"Are you serious? You've been here, what, like a week and a half?"

"What can I say?" I tried to ooze fun and flirtation like Jacinda would. "I am just *that* good."

"What's it for?" The Mercedes' fan belt squealed in protest as he pulled out into the heavy evening traffic.

"It's for this new sunless tanner and, actually, I kind of have to dance around in my underwear like a manic Laker girl with an inner ear problem, so I'd really appreciate it if you could just, you know, not ever watch it. You have TiVo, right? Just skip all commercials from now until July or so. Okay?"

"You're going to be dancing around in your underwear? No way am I going to miss that."

"No, really. It's gonna be boring. Trust me."

"Are you kidding? I'm gonna rig my TiVo to record *just* that commercial."

He smiled and I smiled back, thinking about how good he looked in his navy pullover and jeans. He had these really broad shoulders and really nice hands and . . .

*Stop.* I had to stop this. The last time I'd let my hormones run away with me like this, I'd ended up the school tramp on a plane to Los Angeles. Hadn't I learned *anything?*

"I like your car," I said, trying to sound sincere. "It's really unusual."

He patted the cracked brown dashboard lovingly. "I bought it myself before I left for college. The other guys on the baseball team give me ten kinds of shit about it, but I love this car. Even if it is older than I am."

"How old is it?" I asked, suddenly alarmed that the whole transmission would fall out right in the middle of Beverly Boulevard.

"It's an '81 240 Diesel."

"1981? Are you serious?"

"Yep. Had three hundred fifty thousand miles on it when I bought it and I'm hoping it'll keep running till it hits half a million. I'm restoring it."

I gazed around at the broken sunroof, pockmarked windshield, and ripped seat covers. "That's a big job."

"Yeah, but I'm almost done." His eyes got all misty and lovelorn. My new goal: get him to look at me the same way he looked at this rusty old death trap. "All I have left to do is rebuild the transmission, fix the air-conditioning, hammer the dings out of the body work, replace the master cylinder . . ."

And on and on and on. He'd be finished with his bachelor's degree before he finished working on this car. But his enthusiasm was contagious and I found myself asking questions like, "What's a master cylinder?" and actually being interested in the answer.

When we finally arrived at the parking garage at the Grove, I was starving.

"What do you want for dinner?" he asked, leading me past the upscale shops into the noisy, darkening hubbub of the Farmer's Market. "Mexican? Chinese? Cajun?"

I looked around, taking in the huge array of merchant booths and food stalls. Even if I restricted my options to a fifty-foot radius, I could have my pick of cold beer, tacos, fresh fudge, floral bouquets, and yes, an honest-to-God I "heart" Hollywood T-shirt.

"I don't know," I said slowly. "I have to dance around in my underwear on camera starting tomorrow, so I'm thinking I should stick to a salad." This must be how Coelle felt all the time.

"Sorry." He shook his head. "We're at the cultural food nexus of the universe. You're not having a salad."

"But . . ." I glanced at my upper arms.

"Come on. Don't turn into one of those L.A. salad freaks already." He looked disappointed.

So I gave into my baser instincts and had a big, greasy slice of pizza. And a chocolate donut. (*His* idea. I was being polite.) I would just skip breakfast tomorrow. And lunch. And dinner.

We ate and talked and wandered through the market, stopping to laugh at the kitschy L.A.-themed ashtrays and the tacky postcards. His hand found mine as we headed back toward the shopping center to check movie times but just as I was starting to feel really warm and gushy and buzzed, he said, "I saw your name in the G-Spot on Monday."

My buzz evaporated. Was that damn gossip column mandatory reading for all residents of Los Angeles County? "You did?"

"Yeah, Caleb e-mailed it to me. He wanted me to know how high-profile his new shorty was. But the best part was the 'P.S. In yo face, mouthbreather.'"

I dropped his hand. "I know I come off like a stuck-up snot in that article, but I didn't actually say all that stuff. I was with my roommate, Jacinda, and she gets a little carried away when there's a microphone or a camera in her face."

"I figured." He stopped a few feet from the line at the movie theater. "When you grow up around the business, you find out that a lot of the stuff in the papers is crap. I do have one question, though."

The donut settled in my stomach like a lead weight. "What?"

"Is it true about your dad? That you don't know who he is?"
I nodded.

"You don't want to say anything else about that?"

I shook my head. "There's nothing else to say. Everyone who reads the G-Spot knows as much about it as I do."

He nodded and was reaching over to recapture my hand when a squeaky but outraged voice yelled, *"Hey!"*

I glanced up to see C Money charge out of the theater, dragging a scantily clad redhead behind him.

"No way." I caught Danny's eye and jerked my chin toward his rapidly approaching, frothy-mouthed stepbrother, who today had opted for an understated black jacket and a black leather baseball cap. Worn sideways.

"Here we go." Danny stepped in front of me and braced himself for the confrontation.

"Aha!" Caleb pointed wildly at me, then at Danny. "I caught you! You're caught! Aha!"

"What are you talking about, you caught us?" I asked mildly.

He peered around Danny's shoulder, jabbing his index finger at me. "I caught you cheating on me!"

"*You're* the one who's 'cheating' on me!" I retorted, nodding at his date.

This stymied him for a second, but then he got right back to puffing out his chest. "This ain't about me." Between his crimson face and the black cap, his head looked like a checkerboard. "And she's no one."

"*Excuse* me?" The redhead whapped him in the shoulder with her bejeweled purse. "I'm *no one?*" She turned to me, fury blazing in her eyes. "I'm Riley Sanders, I'm a summer intern with his mom, and yes, he's cheating on you."

"It's okay." I shrugged. "I couldn't care less."

"We hope you two are very happy together," Danny added.

"We *aren't.*" She stalked down the street, then pivoted, stalked back, and shoved a finger in Caleb's face. "Listen up, *ese.* These boots were made for kicking your ass, so you better stay out of my way. I see you again, you're gonna have permanent footprints all over your face."

"Jeez. Don't mess with the redhead in rhinestones, huh?" I said as she marched away.

"L.A. girls are skinny but vicious," Danny said. "It's all that salad—too much lettuce and they turn mean."

C Money started circling Danny, fists up by his chin, yelling, "Let's go, punk! It's on!"

Danny rolled his eyes at me. "You see what I have to live with?"

Caleb's neck veins bulged out. "Mom said you're not supposed to talk to my woman anymore!"

I turned away to hide my smile. *Mom said.*

"Dude, seriously, calm down," Danny urged, clamping a restraining hand on Caleb's shoulder. "This is not cool."

I raised my hand. "And, hi, I'm not your woman."

"That's right." He spat on the sidewalk. "You're a nasty-ass trick, just like yo momma."

That was when Danny hauled off and punched him.

# 19

"Are you *sure* you're okay?" I asked Danny as he parked the car under a streetlight in front of my apartment building.

"For the last time, I'm fine."

We were starting to sound like a broken record, but between the punching and the yelling and the getting thrown out of the Grove, I was feeling a little rattled.

He unbuckled his seat belt and leaned forward to study my face. "Are you okay?"

"Of course." I stiffened. "I think I'll get over Caleb referring to my mother as a 'nasty-ass trick.' I mean, I appreciate you defending her honor and all, but I've heard her called worse."

"I wasn't defending her honor." He reached over and squeezed my hand. "I was defending yours."

"Nina is going to make your life hell when she finds out."

"Let her." He set his jaw, all mulish and defiant. "He can't talk that way about you."

"I'm over it," I assured him. "Really. I don't care. I'm just surprised he was so confrontational. Is he always like that? Do you think he's started taking steroids or something?"

Danny laughed. "Considering he's built like Adrian Brody on heroin, I'm gonna say no. Besides, guys on steroids don't cry when you hit them. What a wuss. I barely even tapped him with my pitching arm—I just had elbow surgery last summer."

I reached for the door handle. "Well, you better come inside. We should put some ice on that lip."

He touched the cut at the corner of his mouth, flinching. "It was that damn diamond pinky ring he always wears. He got one good swing in after the security guy grabbed my arms."

I opened my door and stepped out into the crisp night air. When I looked up at the stars, all I could see was a heavy black blanket of cloud and smog. "Come on. I just hope Jacinda remembered to refill the ice tray after her last hangover."

"I don't need any ice," he insisted, following me onto the sidewalk.

I put my hands on my hips. "Dude. Your bottom lip. Angelina Jolie would be jealous."

Between the swelling and the dried blood, our good night kiss was going to be a tactical nightmare.

"I'm *fine*." He was back on that again. Boys.

As I unlocked the front gate and led him into the courtyard, he said, "I promise there won't be nearly as much street brawling on our next date." Loaded pause. "Assuming you're interested in a next date?"

I executed a saucy hair toss worthy of a Pantene ad. "I might be. But only if you—"

"Eva Cordes. Have you been beating up your date again?" Coelle stuck her head out the front door, waggling her eyebrows at Danny's injury.

"Give me a break. He—"

"We have talked about this and talked about this. Use your words, not your fists."

I gave up on all attempts at flirtation. "Danny, this is my roommate, Coelle. Coelle, Danny."

"Pleased to meet you," Coelle said. "Sorry about that lip. We're working on Eva's anger management skills, but progress has been slow."

Who needs grandparents to humiliate you in front of hot guys when you have "friends"?

"No, she's coming along," Danny replied. "She only backhanded me once and she didn't bite at all."

"Ooh." Coelle looked pleased. "Improvement."

"Ha, ha." I glared at her. *Good night.*

"'Night!" She closed the door, but we could still see her peering through the front window.

"Roommates." He grinned. "Aren't they the best?"

"The best," I echoed, knowing I'd lost any chance of convincing him to come inside.

"Well." He moved in a little closer. "I had a great time tonight."

"Me, too." I was sure he was going to kiss me. I held my breath, puckered up, tilted my head, and waited.

And then . . . nothing.

He squeezed my shoulder, turned on his heel, and headed back toward his car.

What? The hell? Did my breath offend? Had he lost all feeling in his lip? Did my upper arms repulse him?

I decided to blame Coelle. She was about to discover the full extent of my anger management problems.

"He's cute," Coelle said approvingly when I stormed into the apartment. "Very cute. He must work out." She was sprawled on the couch in sweats, her hair in a ponytail and an SAT guide open on her lap.

"Thanks a lot." I slammed the door behind me and threw my purse on the floor. "What the hell was *that?*"

"What the hell was what?" She looked up, Hi-Liter poised in midair.

"Jacinda's out for the night so you're filling in as the resident bitch?" I strode over to the refrigerator and yanked the door open.

"Calm down. I was just saying hello."

*"You ruined my date!"*

"No offense, but it looked kind of ruined already. He was bleeding."

"I thought you were supposed to be the nice one around here."

"I'm the professional one," she corrected. "But it's Friday night, I have nothing to do, and I'm bored."

"Why don't you go wreck your own life, then?"

She threw the Hi-Liter down on the coffee table. "Okay, first of all, my mom already wrecked my life so you don't have to worry about that. Second of all, I wasn't trying to ruin your date. I was just teasing."

"You killed the mood. RIP smoochy, romantic ambience."

She snorted. "Okay, if *that* killed the mood, then the mood must not have been very good to begin with."

"The mood was *great* before you stuck your surgically streamlined nose in. The mood was perfect!"

She closed her study guide. "Are you going to be like this all night?"

I rummaged through the fridge, searching for the leftover mac and cheese I knew I'd left on my shelf. "Don't try to turn this around on me!" I gave up on my shelf and moved to Jacinda's. "And where does all my food keep disappearing to?"

I heard a rustle as she got up from the couch and started toward the stairs. "You know, I thought we could have a good time tonight. We could make popcorn, watch a DVD. I was all ready to give you tips for filming the commercial tomorrow. But now? Forget it. I'm going to bed."

And she did. With her in a snit, Jacinda out with the man she'd had to buy a $2,500 dress to impress, and Danny somewhere at UCLA with a fat lip and no kiss, I had the kitchen and family room all to myself.

Finally. Peace and quiet. I could feel sorry for myself in total solitude.

And that's exactly what I did until quarter to midnight, when my cell rang. Laurel's name flashed on the caller ID.

When I answered, she didn't even bother with "hello." She launched right in with, "Eva Cordes, you better have a good explanation for this."

My mind started racing. "Um. What?"

"I'm only going to give you one chance, so think long and hard before you answer this question: Do you have something to tell me?"

Oh crap. She'd found out about . . . what? My date with Danny? Caleb's black eye? Our plan to break into her house and ransack her file cabinets?

I had a one-in-three shot of correctly guessing the source of her outrage. Not good odds.

So I said the only thing I could. "Nope."

"Really?" Her laugh was sandpapery. "Nothing at all you'd like to disclose?"

"No?"

"All right, then. I gave you a chance to come clean."

A horrible, endless silence ensued.

"Laurel?" I pressed the phone to my ear. "Hello?"

She came roaring back in my ear. "I just checked my voice mail and I had a message from my credit card company. They were concerned about some unusual activity on my card."

Shit.

"So I called their customer service hotline and asked them to read me all the recent charges on my account. And you'll never guess what my balance is."

"Maybe somebody stole your identity?" I croaked.

"You be at my house tomorrow the second the Samba shoot wraps. You're in big trouble, missy. Huge. Think Nixon at the Watergate trials. Janet Jackson at the Super Bowl. Ashlee Simpson and *SNL*."

"I'll be there."

"Damn right you will."

•     •     •

I had to get up at 6:00 on Saturday morning in order to make my 7:00 A.M. call time for the Samba shoot. Jacinda straggled in the front door just as I came downstairs. Her dress was stunning and her face and hair were flawless, but she looked even smaller and shorter than usual, somehow.

"What happened to you?" I asked, shoving a new filter into the coffee maker.

"Nothing." She flung herself onto the couch, one arm over her head.

"Did the dress work its magic?"

"Shut up, okay? I'm too exhausted to talk."

While the coffee was brewing, I darted around the corner to the twenty-four-hour convenience store, where I bought two six-packs of Red Bull (my secret dance elixir) and the new issue of *South of Sunset*. Ever since Gigi Geltin had kicked off the "Guess Eva's Dad, Win Fifteen Seconds of Fame" campaign, I'd read the column religiously. According to my aunt, Gigi should be getting tired of tormenting my mom via unsubstantiated innuendo any day now. "Should" being the operative word. Wednesday's edition had hinted that I'd sprung from the loins of Lenny Kravitz. Which, I mean, come *on*. Besides the fact that my mom had never even met him, wouldn't I have some natural musical ability if my dad were a bona fide rock star–slash–songwriter? Like, I'd at least have made it past the first round of auditions for my high school's chamber singers instead of being begged to stop belting out "Edelweiss" mid-audition?

Jacinda had perked up a bit by the time I returned to the apartment. She'd helped herself to the whole-grain bread I'd toasted, along with a cup of the coffee I'd brewed.

"Hey, is that today's edition?" She peered over my shoulder at the paper, leaving a trail of crumbs on my sleeve.

"Mmm-hmmm." I quickly scanned all the names in bold type. No sign of me or Mom.

"Great. Thanks." She ripped the folded newsprint out of my hand and hunkered down at the kitchen table.

I'd reached the end of my patience with her sticky-fingered selfishness. "Hey, grabby, would you give that back? And as long as we're on the subject, would you please stop pilfering all my food out of the fridge? If it's on my shelf, that means—"

She gasped so loudly I jumped, nearly giving myself a concussion on the cupboard door. "What?"

Her face turned ashen as she started clutching her throat, gasping for breath.

"Jacinda? What's going on? You're freaking me out." I grabbed her arms. "Are you asthmatic? Do you need me to call nine-one-one?"

She wrenched herself free, flung the paper across the room, and bolted up the stairs.

I collected the scattered sections of newspaper and tried to figure out what had sent Jacinda into a code blue.

My gaze fell on this little tidbit:

> My sources report that Skyla Hall, ex-fiancée of nightclub impresario Wyatt Washerton, received the gift that keeps on giving just before she and the notorious playboy parted ways. "She'd bought a Vera Wang gown, booked the caterers, and written her vows," I'm told, but

L.A.'s most elusive bachelor (who just opened the doors to scorching new hot spot Troika) has gotten cold feet six weeks before the walk down the aisle. Skyla didn't leave the relationship entirely empty-handed; Wyatt let her keep her massive diamond engagement ring . . . along with a nasty case of chlamydia. "He's nothing but the poor man's Kevin Federline," sniffs one of Skyla's confidantes, and indeed he has been spotted around town with a blonder, thinner, and younger (!!!) version of Britney Spears—hope she's got a fancy medical plan to match her high-society pedigree!

# 20

"Well, well, well. If it isn't the prodigal niece," Aunt Laurel drawled that evening when I slouched into her dining room. Saturday night at home and she was wearing a black Armani suit. "The latest compulsive shopper in the Cordes clan. How was the shoot, pet?"

"Okay." My whole body ached from grooving frenetically under hot lights all day. The dance routine that had seemed so silly and spontaneous at the audition had gotten old after three solid hours of repetition with only tiny variations. ("Move slower." "Faster." "Sexier." "Not *that* sexy.") "It wasn't as fun as I thought it was going to be."

"That's why they give you a check." She picked up a sheaf of papers emblazoned with the credit card logo and slid her reading glasses up her nose. "Which you're going to need to pay off your mind-boggling debt to Neiman Marcus. Good Lord, Eva, what did you *buy?*"

"I got a little carried away," I mumbled, staring down at the Oriental rug. "I'll pay you back."

"No, really, I'm genuinely curious." She scanned the bill. "What did you treat yourself to that cost roughly the gross national product of a small South American nation?"

Let's see: haircut, highlights, bikini wax, clothes that looked awful on me, clothes that looked okay on me, shoes, purses, my new lucky first-date panties, linens, dinner at Saito (which C Money threw up, what a waste) . . .

"Nothing," I told the floor.

"Hey. Eva. Eye contact, please."

I forced myself to meet her gaze, squirming under the full force of her disapproval. "What do you propose I do about this?" she demanded.

Heat seeped into my cheeks. "I told you, I'll pay you back. You can have my first check from Samba."

Her eyebrows shot up. "And what about the rest?"

"The rest?" Samba was paying me a lot of money.

"Yes. The rest. I wasn't kidding about that small South American nation."

"Well . . . I can work at your agency office."

"Please. Harper will eat you for breakfast and spend lunch and dinner complaining that you were undercooked."

I started to get a wee bit testy. "Well, what do you want me to do?"

She smiled and patted the seat next to hers. "I thought you'd never ask."

I sat down and watched her warily.

"Here." She took off her glasses and lifted her chin toward the ornate silver coffeepot by her elbow. "Have some coffee. Would you like cream or sugar?"

"Neither." Her house was way too quiet and orderly. I finally broke down and asked, "Where's my mom?"

"In Arizona. She was driving me crazy with her constant weeping and wailing, so I sent her to a spa in Scottsdale."

Hey! "So when she's irresponsible, she gets a paid vacation, but if I make a mistake . . ."

"You have to pay the price." She nodded. "That's right. Because it's too late for her, but there's still hope for you."

"How about just this once, I go to the spa and then the next time I screw up, you can punish me double?"

"How about no?"

I shoved back my chair. "Just give me the bottom line, okay?"

"You get right to the point; a girl after my own heart." She folded her hands in front of her. "The bottom line is, I'm going to New York for a few days and I'm giving Veronica the week off."

My heart sank as Rhett poked his head out from under her chair and bared his tiny white teeth at me. "And you need me to take Rhett?" I'd lose at least three fingers trying to clip a leash on that mangy cur.

"Not quite." She shook her head. "Rhett doesn't do well with change—he likes to stay home with his gourmet treats and his filtered water and his orthopedic dog bed. But he's been having a little problem lately. Specifically, he's been pissing all over my house. Veronica took him into the vet yesterday and he has a bladder infection. He's on medication now, but he's been on a peeing spree all over the house for the last week or so."

"So you want me to come over and give him his medicine every day?" I asked hopefully.

"Yes. And I want you to feed him and refill his water twice a day. *And* I want you to go over every inch of carpet, tile, and marble in this house—all six-thousand square feet—and get the urine out. I'll provide the black light, the steam cleaner, the paper towels, and the Nature's Miracle; you provide the elbow grease."

I wrinkled up my nose. "What's the black light for?"

"To help you find the pee stains. If you turn the lights off, the black light illuminates organic material."

"How forensic detective," I said unenthusiastically.

"Now, I want you to steam all of the upstairs carpets, just to be safe, but pay special attention to the stains. The Oriental rugs down here have to be spot-cleaned—you can't steam them. And don't forget to check under the beds, in the closets, all of Rhett's favorite hiding places. Scrub all the floors with the sponge mop in the utility closet. You'll have to move a lot of furniture, but you're a strong girl. It'll be a good workout."

I scowled. "Do you want me to sweep the ashes and darn socks with talking mice while I'm at it?"

"Don't give me any ideas," she warned. "Right now this entire house smells like a poodle puddle and it better be fresh as a friggin' daisy by the time I get home on Friday. And be careful when you're cleaning the marble floor—you can't use vinegar, ammonia, or anything abrasive like a Brillo pad."

I seized on this. "But what if I mess up? What if I accidentally ruin the marble?"

She gave me a piercing look. "Then you'll owe me even more money. Don't try to get out of this."

"I'm not," I lied. "I just—"

"Think of it as a down payment on all the shoes you bought with my money."

My head snapped back up. "Shoes? How did you . . . ?"

She pointed to a charge record on the bill. "Charles David? I'm not stupid, pet, I know what Charles David sells."

"I can wear them to auditions," I said lamely.

"I hope so, because you're going to need a leading role in a Spielberg film to support yourself in the style to which you've apparently become accustomed. Until then, you're on a strict cash allowance." She held out her hand, palm up. "Give me the card back."

"Can't I please have one more chance?"

"Now."

I handed it over, glancing around the dining room. I hadn't truly realized how big this room was. How big *all* of them were. Crawling around this place on my hands and knees, searching for dog pee with a black light, was going to suck hugely.

Except for in the study.

I took a casual sip of coffee and said, "Hey, if I'm going to come by when Veronica's not here, you better give me a key and the alarm code."

"Good point." She picked up the folded newspaper next to her plate and started skimming the headlines. "I'll just give them to you now. Got a pen?"

I wrote down the numbers she dictated and tucked them into my purse, my excitement growing by the second.

"What are you smiling about?" She narrowed her eyes, watching my face intently.

"I'm just excited to spend some time with Rhett. I've, uh, always wanted a dog." Right on cue, he lunged out from under her chair and started attacking my jeans. "What a cutie!"

She melted, scooping up the vicious brute to lavish him with kisses and baby talk. "He *is* a cutie, isn't he? Isn't he? Oh, yes he is! Yes he is! Who's momma's baby? Der he is! Der he is!"

Wait. What happened to the Armani ice queen?

When she finished simpering and calling him by his full doggie name ("Captain Rhett Roo-Roo Sweet Potato Von Pudding Bottom"), she looked more relaxed than I'd ever seen her. I could almost discern a human heart beating beneath all the tailored wool. So I poured another cup of coffee and asked the question that had been bugging me all day:

"Hey, have you ever heard of a guy called Wyatt Washerton?"

"Wyatt Washerton?" She thought a moment, clinking her spoon against her gold-rimmed saucer. "He used to be the king of the young Hollywood party circuit. Kind of like Jacinda is now."

I tried to remain poker-faced. "I see."

"Yeah. He slept with everyone: flight attendants, actresses, supermodels, tennis players. Then he got involved in some shady financial scandal and had to move to Europe, but I heard his lawyers finally worked out a deal and he's moved back to L.A. to try to start a nightclub empire." She chuckled. "He thinks he's Rande Gerber just because he schmoozed at the Viper Room a few times in the nineties."

A horrible thought occurred. "Did he ever date Mom?"

"No. Why?" She tilted her head. "Oh, I get it. This is about finding your dad? Evie, I can say with absolute authority that Wyatt Washerton is *not* your dad. Thank God. Trust me, you wouldn't want to be related to such a slimy sleazebag."

Laurel's housekeeper dropped me off on her way home, and as I walked through the gate of the apartment complex, I ran into Bissy. She was wearing a puffy white parka with white jeans (a definite "don't") and fluffy white mukluks (double "don't").

"Hi there, Eva." She gave me a serpentine smile. "I heard you shot the Samba commercial today."

Thankfully, Mrs. Billington was nowhere to be seen, or I'd be a blood spot on the sidewalk by now. "Yeah. It wasn't . . . I mean, I hardly . . ." I sighed. "Look, Bissy, I'm sorry about what happened at the audition."

"Oh, darlin', it wasn't your fault." But her voice was laced with hostility. "Me and Momma should've known better than to bring the competition along to a callback. And you not havin' a proper family and all, well, I can't hardly expect you to have the same moral upbringing I did."

Maybe I *wasn't* sorry. "Hey. I didn't do anything wrong. They picked me. All I did was pace around the waiting room looking hyper."

That pageant queen smile was still plastered from ear to ear. "Yes, that *is* all you do, isn't it?"

I clapped both hands over my heart. "Ooh, zing."

"You're lucky you're Laurel's niece is all I gotta say." She brushed an imaginary speck off her jacket. "But someday soon, your luck's gonna run out."

"What's that supposed to mean? I should expect to wake up with a severed My Little Pony head in my bed tomorrow morning?"

"You've tangled with the wrong steel magnolia, pumpkin."

I shoved past her and headed into the apartment, where Coelle made a big point of snubbing me. She was curled up on the sofa watching *Animal Precinct,* which she turned up to deafening volumes when I stepped through the door.

"Hi," I ventured. "What's up?"

The volume soared still higher; it now sounded like we had a pack of hungry rottweilers loose in the living room.

"Could you please turn that off?" I hollered. "I want to talk to you."

*Woof, woof, woof.*

"Coelle. Come on. I'm sorry I was such a hag to you last night."

She didn't even glance my way.

"I overreacted. I was upset because Danny didn't kiss me, and I took it out on you."

She blinked. I took this as a sign that I was making headway.

"I'M SORRY I LOST MY SHIT, OKAY?" I screamed just as she turned the TV off.

She tucked her feet under her. "No need to yell. I'll forgive you when I'm good and ready, and not one moment sooner."

In the sudden silence, I could hear the anguished twangs of achy-breaky country music pulsing down through the ceiling.

I pointed upstairs. "Jacinda?"

Coelle nodded. "She's been up there all day, blasting these tragic ballads that could make Barney himself suicidal."

"Well." I sidled over to her. "If you forgive me, I'll make it worth your while. I found out all about the mystery boyfriend."

She remained impassive. "Eh. You were pretty mean."

"This gossip is as juicy as I was crabby last night," I promised. "I'll even throw in lunch at Ürth Caffé."

She mulled this over. "Make it two. Plus you have to pay for parking next time we go to the Beverly Center."

"You drive a hard bargain."

"I'm a child of Hollywood."

"Fine. Am I forgiven?"

"Yes." She nodded her blessing like she was the pope. "Now dish."

I whipped out my fresh copy of *South of Sunset* (I figured—correctly—that Jacinda would have shredded her copy in a fit of apoplectic denial) and pointed out the item about Wyatt Washerton.

"Holy crap," Coelle breathed. "Thirty-five? *Chlamydia?*"

"Hence the suicidal Patsy Cline marathon."

"I wasted two hours of my life in the Neiman Marcus dressing room so this tool could see her in a dress that cost as much as a used car?"

"I know."

"And I should probably know this since I want to go into the sciences and all, but what the hell even is chlamydia? Is that like herpes? Are we talking, like, oozing pustules?"

"Ew." I cringed. "I hope not."

"Hang on." She ran upstairs to grab her laptop. We scoured medical websites for information, then crept up to Jacinda's room.

Coelle rapped on the door. "Hello?"

"Go away!" came a choked, muffled voice.

"We saw the thing about Wyatt," I said. "Is there anything we can do to—"

*"Go away!"*

"I understand what you're going through," I said. "Men are scum—believe me, I know."

"Get out of here before I come out and kick you to death with a sharpened stiletto!"

"Okay, but before we go, do you want anything to eat?" Coelle asked. "I could make a french fry run, if you want."

A long, wet sniffle from the other side of the door. Then: "Fuck off. I don't need pity from a control-freak bulimic and a slut with bad hair extensions."

This had the desired effect—we both backed away from the door.

When we reached the bottom of the stairs, Coelle and I shot questioning glances at each other.

"Bulimic?" I asked. "Really?

"Recovered." She exhaled loudly. "For two years." Then she looked at me. "Slut?"

"Recovered." I shoved my hands into my pockets. "Since November. But . . . how did she know?"

"So how was the commercial shoot?"

Danny called on Sunday night, which, I mean, what the hell? He took me out for pizza and palm tree sunglasses, he took a punch in the mouth for me, he called me afterward, *but he wouldn't kiss me good night?* No wonder every women's magazine devotes like eighty pages to deciphering male language and behavior.

"It went okay," I told him. "I had a little trouble acting sassy and carefree with eighty people and three giant cameras staring at me in my underwear."

"Understandable."

"But then the Red Bull kicked in and I was *en fuego*." I smiled ruefully. "My total humiliation is complete. I just hope I didn't look fat."

"Impossible," he said gallantly. "And hey, at least you got paid, right?"

"In theory." I recapped what had happened with my aunt last night. "A few *minor* indiscretions at Neiman's and she goes nuclear. And get this—I have to spend the rest of the week shuttling back and forth to her house to wait on her beastly little poodle."

He laughed. "Not a dog lover?"

"You don't understand. This is no mere dog. This is a six-pound, red-fanged demon straight from the bowels of hell. With a bladder infection. And guess who has to hand clean all the floors after the little demonette peed all over the place?"

"Maybe the work'll go faster if you put on some music, chug some Red Bull, and start scrubbing in your underwear," he suggested.

"Thanks. That's *so* helpful."

"Well, if you want company, you can always call me," he offered. "I'm done with classes at noon on Tuesday and I'd be happy to help. Especially if you're going to be in your underwear."

See? We'd gone from no kiss to underwear speculation! Where was the magazine article to explain that???

"Forget the underwear. Not gonna happen."

"That's what you say now. But wait until I wow you with my formidable carpet-steaming skills."

"I feel a swoon coming on."

"I get that all the time," he teased. "So it's okay if I come over to help?"

I bit my lip. My aunt never said I *couldn't* invite the guy she'd forbidden me to date over to her house while she was out of town. And we all knew the rules in my family: lying, cheating, and deception were totally acceptable as long as it was "for my own good."

"Sure," I said loftily. "Come on over. It'll be fun."

"E-mail me directions and I'll be there."

"So how was Sunday brunch with Nina and Caleb?" I asked.

"Tense. Nina was . . . let's just say that she and your aunt have a lot in common when it comes to going nuclear."

"What'd she do to you?"

"Ranted, raved, threatened a lawsuit, the usual." He sounded very casual about all this.

"Threatened a lawsuit?" I started gnawing on my lip again. "For what?"

"Assault. But don't worry—she threatens a lawsuit when she gets cut off on the freeway. She's not gonna follow through. Besides, my mom threatened to file a countersuit because of my lip."

"What did your dad do?"

"He chain-smoked cigars for twenty minutes and then yelled at everyone to stop with the lawsuits because he's the one who'll end up having to pay damages and attorney fees and he's already paying too much in alimony. Then my mom threw her bloody mary on him and left."

"Jeez."

"Yeah. We go through that same routine almost every week. But my dad says it's important to spend time as a family. So what did your aunt say when she found out about my beat-down with C Money?"

"She doesn't know yet. But I'll probably have to give Rhett a bath with Evian and brush his teeth when she finds out. Will you still want to date me when I'm an amputee?"


Coelle and I waited until late Sunday night to stage our intervention.

"It's time," she declared, throwing away the uneaten half of her carton of low-cal yogurt. "She's been up there for over thirty-six hours with no food, no phone calls, and no shopping. This is getting serious."

I nodded. "Agreed."

"And I can't stand even one more droopy-ass country song."

"Agreed."

"Here's the plan: I called the free clinic and made an appointment for STD testing tomorrow morning at nine."

"You did?" I grabbed an orange out of the fruit bowl on the counter and started peeling. "God, you're organized."

"I'm the professional one, remember? Now, I don't have to be on the set tomorrow until noon, so we'll both go with her for moral support."

I shook my head. "I don't think she'll want any moral support from me. Why don't you ask someone she actually likes?"

Coelle regarded me with those big, chestnut-colored eyes. "She does like you."

"Uh-huh." I crammed a segment of orange into my mouth.

"I'm sure all that retail hazing and calling me a slut is her way of showing affection."

She stacked her hands under her chin. "You know, Jacinda doesn't have that many friends. Are you going to help or not?"

"I'll help if she'll let me, but don't hold your breath."

"Come on." She led the way upstairs. "I'll unlock the door, you tackle her before she gets a chance to grab any sharp objects."

I paused. "Why don't *I* unlock the door and *you* tackle her?"

"Do you know how to pick a lock?"

My eyebrows shot up. "Do you?"

She nodded, holding up two paper clips that had been straightened out into spindly wires.

"For real? Interesting. Can you open locked file cabinets?"

"Ssh," she whispered as we crept down the hallway. "Don't let her hear you. We need the element of surprise on our side."

I highly doubted she could hear anything over the blaring music, but nodded my assent.

Coelle stuck the wires into the little lock hole, pushed and poked and twisted for a few moments, then tested the doorknob and gave me the thumbs-up. "We're good to go."

I backed up to the end of the hall, pushed off the baseboard, and ran full tilt into the crescendoing guitar twangs as Coelle flung the door open.

# 21

"I despise you both," Jacinda announced the next morning as we tried to get comfortable on the orange plastic chairs in the clinic waiting room. "I just want you to know that."

"We know," I assured her.

"You've made your point," Coelle said. "Loud and clear."

"All right then. Don't be surprised when I have you kidnapped, tortured, and killed next week." She ran her hands over the black wig she'd insisted on wearing, along with dark lipstick and huge, oval sunglasses that covered her face. She'd refused to set foot in a public clinic without a disguise ("I have an internationally famous face and I am *not* about to let Gigi Geltin catch me getting tested for *that disease*"), but her attempt to blend in was attracting the attention of everyone we passed. She looked like Sienna Miller gone Goth.

"You know, this is totally unnecessary," she blustered. "I don't have any symptoms of any kind."

"Good." Coelle pulled a script out of her huge Dolce & Gabbana tote bag and started studying her lines for *Twilight's Tempest*. "But just because you're not getting a giant rash down there doesn't mean you don't have it."

"You are revolting." Jacinda snatched up the waiting room's dog-eared copy of *Newsweek*. "When they make an *E! True Hollywood Story* about me, you are both banned from commentating."

"'Commentating'? Is that even a word?" Coelle didn't look up from her script.

"You tell me, Miss SAT."

"Jacinda, come on." I put a hand on her forearm. "We're just trying to help."

"By assaulting me in the middle of the night and dragging me into the shower with my clothes still on?"

"I warned you not to fight me." I reached up to touch the three-inch scratch she'd left on my neck. Her fingernails should be registered as lethal weapons. Coelle had been right to be leery last night—Jacinda had fought us every step of the way, insisting that she should be left to die of starvation and/or a broken heart, curled up on her bed in her million-thread-count Italian sheets.

"But look at yourself!" Coelle had cried. "Your pedicure is chipped, your hair is greasy, and you smell!"

"Who cares? What's the point of looking good when I'm never leaving the house again?"

We'd had to wrestle her, kicking and screaming, into the shower and turn the hot water on her, fully clothed, while she sobbed hysterically that we were destroying her favorite Blumarine sweats. Then we'd toweled her off, combed her hair, and demanded she go see a doctor.

"I can't," she'd protested. "My parents pay my medical insurance and if they find out about any of this . . ."

So here we were, checking in under a fake name ("Jean Monroe") at the free clinic in Studio City.

"Eva." She dug one of her endless tubes of lip gloss out of her purse. "You can't tell Laurel about any of this."

"Don't worry," I soothed.

"I mean it." She brandished the lip gloss wand like a light saber. "I will—"

"Kill and torture, I heard you the first time. I'm not going to say anything. Promise."

"Why not?" she demanded. "This is your perfect opportunity to get back at me."

"True, but . . ." I cleared my throat. "We're friends, right?"

"I guess." She adjusted her mammoth sunglasses and let the corners of her mouth droop down. "I can't believe I fell for all his stupid lines. He said he loved me, he said I was his soul mate . . ."

"Who?" Coelle tucked a lock of black hair behind her ear. "Patient Zero?"

"Stop calling him that! He has a name, you know: Asshole."

"Of course." Coelle put down the script and rested her chin in her hand. "How many times did you guys do it, anyway?"

"I have the right to remain silent." Jacinda sniffed.

"Didn't they teach you about safe sex in those fancy Swiss finishing schools?" Coelle admonished. "Honestly, how naïve can you be. Always use a—"

"We *did!*" she insisted. "Well, except one time. The condom broke."

Coelle and I exchanged a knowing look.

"Seriously! It broke! I know everybody says that, but I'm telling the truth. God. You don't have to crucify me."

"Nobody's crucifying you." I sat back and took in the many black-and-white posters on the walls promoting sharing your sexual history with your partner and regular prenatal checkups. "We just want to make sure you're okay."

"Well, I'm not okay." She looked wan and sickly under her black wig. "I'm an idiot. Tabloid fodder with scrotty toenails and flat hair."

"You're not an idiot." I nudged her foot with mine. "You were in love. Love makes you do stupid things."

She leaned her head against my arm to commiserate. "Like what happened with you and Bryan?"

"Bryan?" I stiffened. "How do you know about Bryan? I never mentioned him to you."

She rocketed back into an upright position. "I, uh, I meant to say Brynn."

"Who's Brynn?" Coelle wanted to know.

"Brynn is the popular, sadistic tyrant at my old high school. And Bryan was her lacrosse-playing boyfriend. They were the proverbial golden couple."

"Brynn and Bryan?" She gagged. "Vomit."

"I know." I whirled back to Jacinda. "How do you know

about Bryan? And me being a . . . slut?" The description she'd used last night was harsh, but accurate.

"I didn't mean what I said last night," she said. "I was angry, I was lashing out—"

"You know what happened to me in Massachusetts." I caught her gaze and held it. "You know."

She shrugged. "Okay. Maybe I know a little."

"How . . ." My mouth tightened. "Have you been reading my e-mail?"

She hesitated. "No."

I leapt out of my chair. "You did! You hacked into my account and—"

"Child, please. I would never *hack* anything. I might break a nail." She slipped off her sunglasses.

"Well, then, how do you know about Bryan Dufort?"

"Okay. Truth? This guy named Jeff called for you last week—"

"Jeff Oerte?" I started to see red. "My best friend?"

"He didn't *sound* like your best friend. He said you dumped him—"

*"We were never going out!"*

"—for some tool named Bryan who had sex with you to get back at his bitchy girlfriend—"

"Brynn?" Coelle was starting to put the pieces together.

"—and then he told the whole school how trashy you were and never spoke to you again," Jacinda finished. "Is that about right?"

"You forgot the part where Bryan got back together with Brynn and then Brynn and her minions swore vengeance and most of my friends had to stop talking to me to ensure their own survival."

"Except for Jeff," she said, starting to cheer up for the first time in days.

"Jeff?" I laughed bitterly. "Jeff was the worst one. He's ignored me since homecoming—the night of 'The Incident.' And not because of Brynn, just because he's mad."

"He's mad because he's in love with you."

"No, he's not. We've been nextdoor neighbors since kindergarten. He's like my brother."

"Says you." Jacinda exchanged a look with Coelle. "He's totally in love with her. He says he asked you to homecoming and you said no."

"Yeah, because he was cackling like Hannibal Lecter the whole time. I thought it was the setup to some stupid joke."

"Well, trust me. He may be lacking some basic social skills, but he wishes that *he'd* been the one having sex with you."

As much as I tried to block them out, memories of that night came flooding back: the light reflecting off the mirrored disco ball on the polished gym floor; the woodsy spice of Bryan's cologne and the warm pressure of my cheek against his shoulder; the thrilled realization that he had finally noticed me, that someone like *him* would actually want someone like *me* . . . and then, later, the sour taste of warm beer in my mouth, the dizzy nausea and thudding crash into sleep; the groping, the sound of fabric ripping as the zipper of my teal silk dress caught; the long, cold walk home as I clutched my coat around my bare chest.

I shook my head to block out the images and opened my eyes to find both of my roommates gazing speculatively at me.

"What?" Jacinda curled her lip. "Was this Bryan guy bad in bed?"

As long as she knew this much, she might as well know the rest. "I don't know," I said softly.

"Your first time?"

I nodded.

She looked shocked. "Seriously? But aren't you a little old to be—"

*"Jacinda,"* Coelle warned. "You're being supportive, remember?"

"Oh yeah." She dove back into her purse, found some Gummi Bears, and passed the bag around. "Well, I'll let you in on a little secret: if you *don't know* if a guy's bad in bed, he is."

I shook my head. "It's not that simple."

*"Au contraire."* She popped a green Gummi into her mouth. "You would know if he was good. There would be no doubt in your mind."

"No, I mean I don't remember."

Coelle froze midway through refusing the candy.

"Well, babe, if you don't even remember, then he really sucked, no pun intended."

"No, I mean . . ." I sank back down into my chair. "I was kind of drunk."

"How drunk?" Coelle pressed. "Passed out?"

"I guess. We went to this party at his friend's house after the dance and he kept bringing me beer and I was nervous and I wasn't keeping track—"

"And none of your friends were there to help you?"

"Jeff had stomped out the minute Bryan asked me to dance. Besides, it was the lacrosse crowd; my real friends were more . . ." I gave Jacinda a dirty look. "Well, let's just say that *you* would never be seen with any of them. But they were nice and smart and fun and accepting and loyal—well, loyal up to a point; Brynn did a good job of singling me out from the herd."

"Hey, don't get all judgmental with me," Jacinda huffed. "I'm being seen with you right now."

"Yeah, in a wig and bad makeup."

"So what? I would never blow you off just because you had a one-night stand with Bryan Whatever-his-name-was."

"Dufort. So anyway, I drank too much beer, I slept with him, he told the entire lacrosse team every sordid detail, I'm a big fat whore. End of story." I tried to sound casual about the whole thing, but I was cringing inside.

"But you don't remember the actual sex part?"

"Not exactly, but I know my dress was peeled off when I woke up at like three A.M." I hunched over, hiding my face behind my (fake) hair.

"Well, that's *rape!*" Coelle's voice got all strident, like she was about to start picketing outside the supreme court. "That's sexual assault! You can prosecute for that, you can—"

"It wasn't rape," I insisted, hating the sound of the word in my mouth. "I was there. I was a willing participant. I thought he would like me if I, you know . . ."

"We are so stupid." Jacinda dropped the candy back into her purse.

"I know." I hunched lower still. "At least you had a real relationship with a guy who said he loved you. I'm just a pathetic skank."

"Stop talking about yourself that way!" Coelle was getting more agitated by the minute. "It wasn't your fault! He took advantage of you."

"No." I stared down at the scuffed tile floor. "He didn't. I only saw what I wanted to see and forgot all the rules of real life. Guys like him don't have relationships with girls like me."

"What about Danny?" Coelle said. "He's smoking hot and he seems pretty interested."

She was right. Danny was more than smoking hot—he was a good person, which was a lot more than I could say for Bryan Dufort. Danny was the kind of guy I should have waited for; the kind of guy I thought I could never get and now that I had . . .

"Well, it's too late." I straightened up and tried to look impassive. "What happened happened and I can't go back."

"No wonder you don't want to go to Leighton if Brynn's dad is running the place," Coelle said.

"And don't forget her mom is the dean of students. I wasn't about to stay in Alden and let Brynn's whole family beat on me like a rented mule. But even if they hadn't worked there, I had to get out. I couldn't stand one more minute in high school."

"I hear that." Jacinda nodded so hard, her wig nearly fell off.

"So here I am." I turned both palms out. "At a free clinic in the Valley at the crack of dawn with a debutante and a jaded child star. Life in L.A. is *so* glitzy." I turned to Jacinda. "By the way. You said Jeff called?"

"On the landline," she confirmed.

"And he gave you all those details about my life? Just like that?"

She grinned mischievously. "Not exactly. I kind of pretended to be you."

I slammed my fist into my open hand. "Damn you, Crane-Laird."

"Oh, relax, I only fooled him for like three minutes. And after he figured out I was screwing with him, he asked how you were doing and we got to talking and you know me—I can be very persuasive."

"You are Satan in sunglasses," I seethed.

"He sounds nice. And he really misses you. Maybe you should invite him out here and give him a shot—he says he's finally forgiven you for ditching him for that boozy lacrosse player."

"He has a name," I reminded her. "Smegma Boy."

All three of us were giggling when a woman in a white lab coat stepped into the waiting room. "Jean? We're ready for you."

# 23

Laurel had locked all the file cabinets in her study, just as I feared. So I had no choice but to call in reinforcements (a.k.a. Coelle) on Tuesday, even though I'd wanted to spend some alone time with Danny.

Correction: Before I started scrubbing, I'd wanted to spend some alone time with Danny. I'd had this warm, fuzzy vision of us mopping up the kitchen together, kissing and flicking bubbles at each other like some hilarious Home Depot commercial. But by the time he showed up at one o'clock, I'd already put in four solid hours of carpet steaming and I no longer wanted Pine-Sol foreplay; I just wanted help. My forearms were throbbing, my shoulders were screaming, and my ankles were covered with tiny toothmarks from Rhett's surprise attacks.

"Hallelujah!" I dropped the hand steamer and ran down to the foyer when the doorbell finally rang.

"I come bearing Krispy Kremes," Danny announced when I opened the door.

His smile? So adorable. His hands? So manly. The donuts? So delicious. "My hero. Come on in."

The scent of freshly mowed grass wafted into the foyer as he stepped inside. I could hear the faint buzz of a lawnmower coming from the mansion next door. "So how goes the battle?" he asked, glancing at the sheen of sweat glossing my forehead.

I wiped my brow with the sleeve of the Blumarine sweatshirt I'd swiped from Jacinda (hey, as long as it was already ruined . . . ). "Not good. This house is gigantic and that dog might weigh six pounds, but four pounds of that must be bladder capacity."

Right on cue, Rhett pranced into the entryway, yipping at the top of his tiny lungs.

"There's the little monster now," I said.

Rhett bounded up to Danny, tail wagging, eyes dancing, and rolled right over for a belly rub.

Danny knelt down to oblige. "*This* is the killer dog that terrorizes you?"

"Just wait. He'll take a chunk out of your hand any second."

But Rhett wasn't finished with his Benji routine. He wiggled with delight while Danny petted him, then raced into the kitchen and brought back a filthy old rubber ball, which he dropped at Danny's feet.

"Yeah, he's bloodthirsty, all right." Danny picked up the ball and tossed it down the hallway. Rhett shot after it, barking joyously.

"That's not his real personality," I swore. "You'll see."

He tried to look grave. "I *want* to believe you, but . . ."

"Come on." I reached up to rub my aching neck and nodded at the steam cleaner. "Grab some Nature's Miracle; these rugs ain't getting any fresher."

"What's wrong with your neck?" he asked.

"Carpet cleaning is tough on the spine. But I just popped three Advil so I should be getting my second wind any minute now."

He put down the donuts on the glass-top table. "Do you want a shoulder rub?"

Does a miniature poodle pee in the walk-in closet? "Yes, please." The kissing-and-bubble-flicking fantasy was suddenly making a comeback.

But he had stopped focusing on me, having been transfixed by the two-story mural of the barefoot peasants in the Tuscan vineyard.

He stared up, open-mouthed. "That painting . . . is so . . ."

"Hideous? I know." I started down the hall and motioned for him to follow me. "Wait until you see what's in the family room."

"Dude." Danny gaped up at the wall.

"I told you."

"I mean, who would actually pay to . . . ?"

"Some action hero from the eighties who missed Mother Italy."

The golden afternoon sunlight poured in through the windows, making the world's ugliest painting look even uglier.

Danny couldn't look away from the gondolier singing under

a full moon with the Leaning Tower of Pisa (with the Roman Colosseum in the background). *"Wow."* He blinked about fifty times in a row.

"Wait. It takes a few minutes for the full effect to sink in."

"Whoever painted this should be arrested for vandalism. Or assault with acrylic. *Something.*"

We stood side by side, heads tilted back, marveling at the extravaganza of gaudiness. Suddenly, his arm was around my waist. I leaned in, but we didn't look at each other. We kept our eyes on the mustachioed gondolier, his jaunty red bandanna, and the crumbling Roman amphitheater behind the flooded canal.

And then we were kissing. I wasn't sure exactly what prompted it—there weren't any sexy shoulder massages or cheesy lines about "I think I have something stuck in my eye— won't you take a real close look?" and the pink-faced gondolier had zero aphrodisiac appeal—but in the space of two seconds we went from staring at the wall to pressing our lips together as if we were performing lifesaving CPR.

CPR with a lot of tongue. I was hardly an expert at French kissing, but the amazing thing was, I didn't have to pretend to be blasé or worry about whether I was moving my lips too much or too little. I actually relaxed and lost myself in the kiss and I could tell he did, too.

We kissed and kissed, our bodies plastered together, inching ever so slowly toward the couch.

When I came up for air, unwanted memories surged up in my mind—vague impressions of warm beer and ripping silk and shame curdling in my stomach—but I tamped them down and kissed Danny harder. I wanted to forget that homecoming had ever happened.

He kissed me back, warm and slow.

Then the doorbell chimed again.

"My roommates," I whispered thickly.

"They'll go away." He leaned over and kissed the side of my neck, right under the jawline. *Ooh.*

"Hey!" Frenzied knocking at the door. "We know you're in there! We will not be ignored!"

"That's Jacinda." I pulled away reluctantly.

"You guys are making out in there, aren't you? Put your clothes back on and let us in!"

"She's very perceptive," Danny muttered.

"She's very *annoying.*"

"We want in! We want in!" Two sets of fists pounded in time to the chanting.

"I better open the door before the neighborhood security guard shows up," I said. "And if one of them should happen to die in a carpet-steaming malfunction, remember: it was an accident."

"You're going to get it when Laurel finds out you were getting frisky with the Forbidden One in her house," was how Jacinda greeted me when I opened the door.

"We were not 'getting frisky,'" I blustered.

"Liar, liar, Brazilian thong on fire."

"You *do* look flushed." Coelle winked at me as she followed Jacinda in. "You sure you weren't getting a little something-something?"

I tapped one flip-flop–clad foot on the marble floor. "If I wanted to be singled out and harassed, I'd go back to high school."

"No, you wouldn't," Jacinda scoffed. "Maybe we're a little snarky, but at least we don't make you take exams or write papers on the most boring book in the world."

"*Walden?*" Coelle guessed.

"Bingo."

"Why can't high schools teach any of the things we really need to know?" I wondered. "Like how to deal with moms who wish they'd never had you. Or how to tell if the lacrosse player who asked you to dance is just using you to make his girlfriend jealous."

Coelle nodded. "How to calculate how much longer a car ride to Santa Monica is going to take if it's rush hour."

"How to budget with a credit card."

"How to tell if you have chlamydia." Jacinda gritted her teeth.

"Hey, did the doctor call yet?" I asked. She'd been sent home from the clinic yesterday with a bunch of reproductive health pamphlets and a promise that she'd get a call as soon as her test results returned from the lab.

"Not yet. But I called every single PR contact I have, and trust me, Asshole's hot new clubs aren't going to be hot for long. He'll never get a mention in *Us Weekly* or Page Six again."

"Hell hath no fury like a socialite scorned," Coelle said as Danny ambled into the foyer, Rhett tagging along after him like a devoted, well-trained puppy.

"Hel-lo," Jacinda singsonged as she rushed over to inspect the fresh meat.

"Danny, this is my roommate, Jacinda. And you've met Coelle."

"Hi again." Coelle flashed a quick smile before turning to glare at Jacinda, who was in full pouty-lipped, boob-jutting, eyelash-batting mode. "Knock it off. He's taken."

"I know." She dropped the sexpot routine. "I'm just saying hi."

Danny grinned at me. "I'm 'taken'?"

I could feel the blush seeping from my bangs all the way down to my toenails. "I'm mortified."

"Oh, what a darling little poodle!" Coelle leaned down to scratch Rhett behind the ears and he lunged for her, gnashing his teeth.

"Whoa." She snapped upright. "What's wrong? Fear aggression? Did I make eye contact too soon?"

I shot Danny an I-told-you-so look. "No, he was just born vicious."

Jacinda had no tolerance for small talk that didn't revolve around her. "Hel-lo! I'm here, I'm a woman in demand, I don't have all day. Let's get to work."

Danny, assuming she meant carpet duty, regarded her with newfound respect. "Okay. Why don't you guys start with the tile floors in the kitchen and the hall and Eva and I will finish the upstairs . . ."

He trailed off as Jacinda, Coelle, and I exchanged a flurry of meaningful looks. "What?"

"Nothing," I said a little too quickly. "I just think that, you know, it might be better if the three of us work together."

"Yes!" Coelle agreed. "Like on the Oriental rug in the, oh, say the study. It's very delicate work and she can show us exactly what to do."

"Morale will be higher if we stick together," Jacinda agreed.

"And you're so big and strong, you can steam the rest of the up-stairs in no time."

He looked utterly confused. "Morale?"

"Yeah." We all nodded.

"Okay. It's settled." Coelle located the utility closet, where she gathered up an assortment of paper towels, buckets, and spray-on spot cleanser. "We'll be in Laurel's study if you need anything."

"We'll meet you in the kitchen for a Krispy Kreme break in half an hour." I couldn't quite look him in the eyes as we backed into the hallway and closed the heavy pocket door.

"Great. He thinks I'm blowing him off, you know," I hissed at my roommates as we raced toward the living room.

"Why don't you just tell him what we're really up to?" Jacinda asked.

"Because one, I don't want him to think I make a habit of criminal activities. Two, I have no idea what we're going to find and until I do, no one else needs to know about this."

"Well, just do whatever you were doing to him when we first rang the doorbell and he'll get over it."

"Yeah. Do you want to smooch some guy you just met two weeks ago or do you want to find out the truth about your dad?" Coelle asked. "Get your priorities straight."

"Hurry up—let's get this over with," I urged.

We opened the door to Laurel's study and gazed in at the dark wood paneling. Jacinda strode purposefully toward the far wall. "I'll take the filing cabinet."

"You can't; most of them are locked. I checked already."

Coelle whipped two paper clips out of her jeans pocket and

started flattening out the wires. "Give me three minutes."

Precisely three minutes later, we were thumbing through neatly filed rows of manila envelopes. Lots of contracts and investment reports and legal documents, but nothing about my mom.

"Where else would you keep important papers?" Coelle mused.

"If she put 'em in a safety deposit box at the bank, you're screwed," Jacinda informed me.

"Way to think positive." I ran my hand along the cool, polished desktop, checking for clues. "All of her desk drawers open, except the bottom one."

"You think that's where she keeps the juicy stuff?" Coelle finessed the lock with her paper clips, but it wouldn't open. "This one's tricky." Her face twisted up in concentration. "Come *on,* you stupid, stubborn . . ."

"Step aside, ladies, step aside." Jacinda pulled a bobby pin out of her hair and headed toward the desk. "Professional coming through."

"A bobby pin?" Coelle smirked. "You can't be serious. That only works for Nancy Drew and the Hardy Boys."

"Says the amateur with the paper clip. Prepare to be amazed." She stuck the pin into the small keyhole, wiggled it around for a few seconds, and then, voilà, the drawer slid open. "Smack my ass and call me Nancy."

I stared at her. "How . . . ?"

"You don't want to know. Let's just say I got kicked out of schools for a reason and leave it at that."

I thumbed through the manila folders that Laurel had labeled in her straight, blocky handwriting. Taxes, travel receipts, check stubs . . .

"Nothing," I reported, my heart sinking. "Just more financial papers."

"Are you sure?" Jacinda peered over my shoulder.

"Hang on." I yanked the drawer out as far as it would go, looking for a label reading "Eva" or "Marisela" or "The deep, dark secrets of my niece's illegitimate parentage."

But no such luck.

Maybe my aunt *had* put the really confidential stuff in a safety deposit box. How would we ever manage to break into a bank vault?

And then I saw it. Tucked waaay in back, behind the dozens of identical manila folders, was a patch of red. I reached in, grabbed for the last folder, and tugged it out.

The crimson file had only two words written on the label: HEAD SHOTS. Sure enough, when I opened the cover, several glossy photos of my mom spilled out on to the carpet. She looked younger, happier than she did now. You'd never guess, looking at the confident brunette glamazon in these pictures, that she'd end up broke, alone, and semi-addicted to everything from vodka to Vivienne Westwood.

I hit pay dirt behind the photos. Laurel had scrupulously kept copies of Mom's passport and driver's license circa 1985, and—cha-*ching!*—some personal correspondence. Apparently, my mom hit the big time before e-mail was invented, because most of her notes to Laurel were scribbled on gaudy, pretentious sheets of stationery with swirly monograms and gold etching.

"Here we go. I found something." I sifted through the letters, trying to figure out when they were written—Mom being Mom, she hadn't dated anything.

The first few started out like this:

*Laurel—*

*I know you said not to ask for any more money, but this really is an emergency . . .*

*I'm in Paris, I'm hungover, but I finished the shoot yesterday. Didn't I tell you I'd be on my best behavior? And if Rosalie calls to tattle about my slapping that horrid little wardrobe assistant, just be aware that I was PROVOKED . . .*

*L—I tried to break it off with Simon, but he got so distraught and I couldn't bear to see him suffer. You know how sensitive musicians are and he only cheated on me the one time, so . . .*

"Simon," I murmured, grabbing a pad and pen off my aunt's desk. I wrote down the name so I could research it later.

As it turned out, I didn't have to. The next note read:

*Thanks for the flowers. They were by far the most gorgeous in the maternity ward, and you know how I love my lilies. Eva is tiny and perfect and a miracle. She's going to be gorgeous, just like me!*

*No word from Mom and Dad, of course, not even a phone call. And nothing from that #@%^* bastard Anatole*

*Farnsworth. Would you have your lawyer call his lawyer*
*and ask if he plans to even acknowledge his own daughter?*

At the bottom of the page, she'd drawn a little cartoon baby with wings and a halo.

"Oh my God." I sat down heavily.

They both rushed over to read the note over my shoulder.

"Anatole Farnsworth," Jacinda mused. "Why do I feel like I've heard of him?"

"Do you know him?" I demanded. "What's he like?"

"That name sounds really familiar," Coelle chimed in. "But I don't know why." She pointed at the notepad in my hand. "Write it down."

"I don't need to write it down," I said. "I'll remember."

Finally, I had proof. Proof of my father's identity, proof that my mother had loved me once upon a time.

And then I noticed the next letter in the batch:

*Laurel—*
*I know it's been a long time since we talked, but I desper-*
*ately need help. You have to return my phone calls. You*
*HAVE to. Because, well, there's no good way to say this. I'm*
*pregnant again.*

"No way." I turned the letter over and over, searching for any sign of what came next. "I'm not an only child?"

# 24

"What?!? Are you serious?"

"Move over. Let me see!"

My roommates crowded into the corner behind the desk, peering over my shoulder.

"It's from my mom." I waved the letter at them. "She got pregnant again after she had me!"

Coelle's eyes bugged out. "And this is the first you're hearing about it?"

"Yeah!" I tried to think coherent thoughts, but nothing doing. "I can't believe this!"

"Well, what happened to the baby?" Jacinda, still in full Nancy Drew mode, squinted down at the messy scrawled handwriting. "You're sure your mom never mentioned anything to you?"

I just gave her a look.

"Okay, stupid question."

"I hate her." I slammed my palm down on the floor. "I *hate* her."

"Don't worry." Coelle squeezed my arm. "We'll figure everything out. So if she got pregnant one more time after you—"

"One more time *that we know of,*" I spat out.

"—and you're an only child . . ." She scrunched up her mouth and looked at me pityingly. "Well. Maybe she had an abortion."

"Or maybe she gave the kid up for adoption," Jacinda chimed in. "Or maybe she miscarried. Who knows?"

"Laurel knows," I snapped. "That's who. Another lie she went along with to 'protect' me."

"Is there anything else in that folder?" Coelle wrested the letters away from me. "Anything else that might—"

"Eva?"

We all gasped as Danny stepped into the doorway.

"Danny. Hi!" I struggled to my feet. "You startled me."

He stared at me for a few seconds, then glanced down at the rug. "I thought you guys were working in here?"

"We were." I leaned back against the desktop in what I hoped was a nonchalant fashion. "I mean, we are. I mean, we're just taking a little break to . . . you know . . ."

He looked at me. "This is about finding your dad, isn't it?"

"Um. Possibly."

"If you wanted help, you could've just asked me."

I finally made eye contact. "I know, but what if . . . ?"

"Eva. I would never tell anyone anything. You can trust me."

"Ooh, cute *and* trustworthy," Jacinda gushed.

"Definitely a keeper," Coelle whispered.

He squished in behind the desk with the rest of us. "What have you found so far?"

Two weeks later . . .

From: lacrosse_king69@freshyfresh.net <Bryan Dufort III>
To: OutOfEden@globecon.com <eva cordes>
Subject: saw you on TV
Hey Eva—
I heard that you did some commercial, but I didn't believe
it till I saw it during the football game last night. You
looked sexy. Way more sexy than Brynn. (I'm breaking up
with her after graduation.)
Are you coming back to Alden this summer? We could fin-
ish what we started at homecoming. You know I'll blow
your mind. I bet you learned some hot new tricks in Los
Angeles.
Call me when you're ready to party: 413-555-8665.
Bryan

From: OutOfEden@globecon.com <eva cordes>
To: descartesismybizatch@wordup.net <Jeff Oerte>
Subject: FWD: saw you on TV
Jeff—
So good to finally talk to you last week. I'm glad Jacinda
beat some sense into you.
I'm forwarding along a very touching and sensitive e-mail
I got from Smegma Boy. Try to hold the tears back when
you read it.
What do you think I should do? Sign him up for a date

rape awareness mailing list and a bunch of Viagra spam?
Or just ignore?
E.


From: descartesismybizatch@wordup.net <Jeff Oerte>
To: OutOfEden@globecon.com <eva cordes>
Subject: RE: FWD: saw you on TV
E—
I have a better idea. I'll call you tonight and give you the
details. What's your cellphone number? (Jacinda is scary.)
Jeff

# 25

I asked Jacinda for flirting tips and Coelle for acting tips before I dialed the phone. If I was going to pull this off, I had to strike just the right balance of slutty and sophisticated.

Jacinda, who had been declared officially chlamydia-free last week, suggested I drink a whole bottle of red wine before making the call. "That always puts me in a come-hither mood."

Coelle had bonked her on the head with an empty soda can. "Yeah, but she's gotta be able to think on her feet. She can't do that right after she chugged a whole bottle of wine, idiot."

"Well, do you have a better idea, oh great method actor?"

Coelle had smiled smugly. "Actually, I do."

"She has no idea how to be flirty," Jacinda warned me. "The only guy who's asked her out in the last six months is a stalker from prison in Joliet, Illinois."

"It's not my fault I'm busy and inmates love *Twilight's Tempest!*" Coelle harrumphed, picking up her SAT study guide. "Eva, if you want to sound flirty, *do* something flirty, like putting on makeup. Applying mascara not only primes your mood; you naturally open your eyes and mouth into a surprised expression, which keeps your voice high and coquettish."

"Co*what*ish?" Jacinda seized the study guide. "Gimme that."

I had left them downstairs to bicker and locked myself in the bathroom where, as per Coelle's advice, I broke out my cellphone and a tube of mascara.

I punched in the number, held my breath through the first two rings, then whipped out the mascara wand and started to coat the lashes of my left eye.

"'Lo?" His voice was deep and smooth and confident—he *sounded* good-looking, even from three thousand miles away.

I exhaled slowly and forced my voice into a light tease. "Hi, Bryan. Do you know who this is?"

He laughed nervously. "Brynn?"

I switched to the right eye. "Nooo."

"Kayla?" he guessed.

"Nope."

"Emily?"

I frowned. Was he too lazy to even check his caller ID? "It's Eva. Eva Cordes."

"Oh, Eva." He perked right up. "Hey."

"I got your e-mail." I tried to force out a giggle. "You are *bad.*"

"Yeah, I know." I could hear the grin in his voice.

"I can't believe you're gonna break up with Brynn. I thought you two would be together forever."

"Nah. I mean, we had fun and all, but—"

"Oh, I know how fun you can be," I oozed. I was gonna need five hot showers after we finished this conversation.

"Yeah, we had a good time at homecoming, didn't we?"

I caught my reflection in the mirror and forced my facial muscles out of their savage glower and back into the open-mouthed mascara expression.

"Absolutely," I agreed. "But after what happened with Brynn, I was surprised to hear from you."

"Seeing you dancing around in that commercial . . ." his voice trailed off and I tried not to think too hard about what he might be doing on his end of the line. "I'll break up with Brynn in a second if you're coming back to Alden."

"Ooh, you will? Really?"

"Are you kidding? For a girl who's hot enough to dance in lingerie on national TV?"

I had to break character for a moment. "Well, actually, they were boy shorts. And a tank top. That's not really the same thing."

"Who cares? You were brutally hot. I didn't know you could move like that. You used to be so quiet and stuff. So what's the deal? When are you coming back for a little visit?"

"Soon," I promised. "Soon. So listen. Bryan. When you said we could 'finish what we started' this summer . . . what'd you have in mind for round two?"

The nervous laughter was back. "Well, this time I could, you know . . ."

"I don't know," I purred. "Tell me. Tell me exactly what you're going to do to me."

"Well, this time, heh heh, we could actually, you know, *do it* instead of passing out on the futon."

My heart started thudding around my rib cage. "So we didn't . . . we never . . . you passed out before we actually finished?"

More heh heh-ing. "God, you *were* drunk, weren't you?"

"I was unconscious," I spat. "I was unconscious and you were groping me and ripping my dress off."

"Yeah," he said cheerfully. "I took your dress off and then the Jäger shots hit me like a Mack truck and next thing I knew, I woke up in a pool of puke and you had gone home."

I threw the mascara tube across the room. *"Then why the fuck did you tell Brynn and every single guy on the lacrosse team that I had sex with you?"*

"Don't get upset, baby. It'll be better next time."

*"If you ever call me 'baby' again I will gut you like a red snapper, do you hear me?"*

He paused. "Are you mad?"

"I'm a homicide waiting to happen."

"But . . ." he sounded confused. "We're still gonna party this summer, right? Make sure you bring the br— I mean, the tank top and the boy shorts you wore in that commercial, okay?"

"Go to hell!"

"What? Wait . . ."

"I hope Brynn cheats on you and gives you chlamydia."

"Eva, come on. You like me. I know you do."

"I liked you before I knew what a real man was," I shot back.

"Hey—"

"You are going to tell Brynn and every other single person at Alden High School that you lied about what happened after homecoming. In fact, you're going to tell them that we never even kissed—that you made the whole thing up."

"But we did kiss!" he protested. "I remember that part!"

"Yeah, you're such a stickler for the truth." My laugh came out short and harsh. "You tell them you made the whole thing up."

"No." Even when confronted with his inherent scumminess, he remained supremely confident. "Next time I tell the story, you're going to be even sluttier."

"You apologize!" Jeff, who had managed to remain silent on the third-party line I'd beeped in before calling Danny, could hold back no longer. "I'm going to kick your ass, Dufort!"

"Who's that?" Bryan demanded.

"It's Jeff Oerte—the guy who's going to *kick your ass* tomorrow."

"Calm down, Jeff," I warned.

But we were way past the point of calming down. "Apologize to Eva right now!"

"This is stupid. I'm hanging up," Bryan announced.

"You go right ahead," I said silkily. "But before you do, I just wanted to let you know that we've recorded this entire conversation and we are going to send the tape, along with the e-mail you sent me yesterday, to Brynn."

"And maybe Emily and Kayla, too," Jeff threw in.

"Let me tell you a little something about your perfect, gorgeous girlfriend: she is a master of psychological torture. I've experienced her skills firsthand. And she knows you a lot better than she ever knew me; she'd probably break out the really sadistic tricks for you."

"Apologize!" Jeff barked. "Right now."

"I . . ." Bryan's voice quavered as if near tears. "I'm sorry, Eva. Don't send anything to Brynn. I'm sorry."

A totally insincere apology, but better than nothing.

"And?" I prompted.

"And . . . I'll tell everyone I made the whole thing up."

"You better, or Brynn's gonna get a little surprise package."

He clicked off the line, leaving Jeff with no outlet for his macho outrage.

"What a tool."

"I know."

"I could *totally* kick his ass, you know."

I smiled. Pasty math guy versus the lacrosse king. "I know."

"And, Eva? I'm sorry. I shouldn't have been so . . . I was just mad because I . . . well, because I wanted to . . ."

My smile turned wistful. "I know. I'm sorry, too."

"Maybe it's not too late?"

I didn't answer.

"You could come back now, you know." He sounded hopeful. "You could finish senior year with the rest of us. Brynn will leave you alone. Come on, Alden needs you."

# 26

"So this is it?" I looked around in disbelief. "The most romantic spot in all of Los Angeles?"

Danny nodded. "The most *nonclichéd* romantic spot. I could have taken you up to Mulholland or Zuma Beach, but we'd have to wait in line behind all the other hormone-crazed couples to see the view. You have to get creative if you want any privacy in this city."

He'd driven for what felt like hours until he finally pulled onto an unassuming little side street in the beachside neighborhood of Playa del Rey. The road twisted and turned through flat, scraggly patches of grass and concrete walls until it drew up alongside a chain-link fence topped with barbed wire.

And behind the chain-link fence? The runway for LAX.

We'd stopped at an In-N-Out drive-thru for burgers, fries, and drinks, which we had spread out on the hood of the car.

"You're sure this is romantic?" I said, trying not to sound too skeptical. "Airbuses and seven-forty-sevens? You know, people pay good money to *not* live under airport flight paths."

"You'll see." He took off his baseball cap, the better to survey the darkening horizon.

I fidgeted for a few seconds, full of things to say. "My friend Jeff wants me to come back to Alden."

He raised an eyebrow. "I think your friend Jeff has a little crush on you."

I sipped my chocolate shake. "It doesn't matter, anyway—my grandparents moved to Florida, so I wouldn't even have a place to live."

"But if they still lived there, you'd go back?" He touched his left elbow—his pitching arm—which I'd seen him do when he was nervous or hurt.

"No," I said firmly. "I mean, apparently, I'm going to have a fabulous career in freestyle underwear dance. And I have to find out more about my father."

His expression of hurt changed to surprise. "You haven't investigated yet?"

"No." I ducked my head. "I know that all I have to do is go online and look up his name, but I just can't. My whole life I've been dying to know, and now that I finally have a name, I'm wimping out. It doesn't make any sense."

"You want to know, but you don't want to know."

"Yeah. I'm scared. I mean, what if Jacinda's heard the name because he's a serial killer or something? What if he's even worse than my mother? I know that's hard to imagine, but I guess it's *possible*."

"You'll find out when you're ready."

"When I was little and my mom wouldn't call or come to visit, I used to imagine that I had this great father out there who would, like, take me fishing and whatever, if only he knew I existed. He would be this perfect, handsome Disney movie dad." I put aside my shake. "Pretty stupid, huh?"

"You'll find out when you're ready," he repeated. "But back to my question: What else is keeping you from going back home? Your career, your parents . . . anything else?"

I winked. "Maybe."

"Like what?"

"Well." I wrinkled up my forehead. "I still have to make friends with Rhett, poodle of death."

"And . . . ?"

"And Jacinda and Coelle might come around someday, too."

His breath was warm against my ear. "One more chance."

I laughed. "And there's this guy . . ."

"Really."

"Mm-hmm. He's older, athletic, and, oh yeah, *forbidden*."

"Good-looking?"

"Eh." I dissolved in giggles as he pinned me to the car hood and tickled me into submission. "Okay, okay, he's good-looking. Prince William in a baseball cap."

He let me up. "And he's way better than that guy Jeff?"

I fluttered my eyelashes. "Totally. He takes me to the *most* romantic places. Sometimes they don't even smell like jet fuel."

More tickling, more giggling, and more kissing. A lot more.

As the red-streaked sunset faded into night, I curled up next to him, both of us reclining on the cool glass of the windshield. I took a deep breath, inhaling lingering fumes of gasoline mixed with sea breeze, and finally relaxed as the first jet arrived.

The engine noise drowned out all attempts at communication, which was unfortunate, given that I had a few moments of horrified certainty that the huge hunk of metal was going to land directly on top of us.

"We're gonna die!" I screamed directly in Danny's ear. He couldn't hear me, but that didn't stop me from continuing to yell.

We didn't die, of course; we both started laughing, even though we couldn't understand what the other was saying. His arms were wrapped around me, anchoring me amid the total sensory overload. A sudden hot wind blew my hair back against my face. I stopped trying to talk and gave myself over to the power and potential roaring through me.

"I'm not going back home," I whispered, even though I knew he couldn't hear me over the thunderous din. "I *am* home."

Look for

# the 310:
# EVERYTHING
# SHE WANTS

coming from MTV Books
in August 2006

Turn the page for a sneak preview. . . .

Even the door knocker was intimidating.

This just seemed like overkill to me. I mean, I'd already had to get past the Frenchified ceramic plaques announcing the entrance to Bel Air, the narrow, foliage-lined roads full of hair-pin turns, and the staticky intercom mounted by the entrance to a brick-paved driveway—complete with freshly washed Rolls Royce—to get to the house.

Let me just say that the Farnsworth estate made Aunt Laurel's posh Bev Hills digs look like a double-wide trailer in Arkansas. This house was straight out of a European history textbook—think Palace of Versailles; the kind of sumptuous spread that could accommodate a temperature-controlled wine cellar, a private screening room, an indoor lap pool, and an underground bowling alley.

Not, of course, that my father and his family would ever sully themselves with anything so tacky and pleb as bowling. They probably spent their leisure time playing polo and yachting, kicking back with mint juleps, lamenting how hard it was to find good help these days, and braying, "I say, old chap . . ."

But I shouldn't be so quick to judge. They were, after all, my family. And they *had* agreed to meet me for lunch. I had an invitation from Mrs. Daphne Farnsworth herself. My father's wife. My mother's nemesis.

"She wants you to come by for lunch on Thursday," Laurel had said, looking like there was a lot more to this announcement. "You don't have to go."

"Of course I'm going. What should I wear?"

She gave me a hard look. "A bulletproof vest."

I'd opted for a slightly more subtle outfit—a modest white sweater and a fluttery Diane von Furstenberg skirt I'd borrowed from Coelle. I'd even put on some pearl earrings. How demure.

I'd also hounded Jacinda for finishing school tips—even if she wasn't using them, at least one of us could act like a lady. What was the high society–approved way to hold my knife? Unfold my napkin? Eat cucumber sandwiches with the crusts cut off?

"I got nothing." She'd shrugged when I quizzed her on all this. "All I learned in finishing school was how to cheat on exams and get rid of empty vodka bottles without anyone noticing."

So I'd walked down to the bookstore, bought *The Idiot's*

*Guide to Etiquette,* and crammed on the continental style of dining and how to write the perfect monogrammed thank-you note. Bring on the cucumber sandwiches!

I looked around the mansion's ornately carved stone archway, but couldn't locate a doorbell. So I took a deep breath, grabbed the heavy brass door knocker, and rapped twice.

Nothing happened.

Just as I was about to whip out my cell, call Aunt Laurel and ask her to make sure we'd gotten the day right, the door swung open, revealing a majestic foyer.

A liveried butler ushered me in without a hint of a smile, announced, "Madam will be with you shortly," then took off down the hall. My eyes darted around the marble pillars, abstract sculptures, and holy crap, was that a real Picasso?

The sharp staccato of high heels on marble echoed around me as Mrs. Daphne Farnsworth approached. I could tell she had been beautiful once, but now she looked skeletal and wrinkly. She was decked out in a tweedy Chanel suit with a string of huge, lustrous gray pearls around her throat. Her silver hair was pulled back in a loose chignon.

I knew I should introduce myself, but I was too terrified to even squeak out a hello.

Her blue eyes glittered as they raked over me; I was acutely aware that my outfit was borrowed, my shoes were cheap, I didn't belong in this lavish, silent world.

"You must be Eva?" She smiled, an effort which seemed to cause her physical pain because it came out more of a grimace.

I nodded wordlessly.

She reached out to take my right hand in both of hers. Her

skin felt smooth and crinkly and cool. I finally started to relax.

"Yes, you're Anatole's daughter. I can see it in the chin and the eyes."

At last! Someone to blame for my cavernous Precious Moments eye sockets. But I was glad to know that I looked like him, that people could tell I fit into a family. So I smiled back.

"Will I meet everyone today? The whole family?" I asked, trying not to sound pathetically eager.

Her smile hardened while her eyes gleamed even brighter. "Won't you please wait here a moment?"

She clicked back down the hall and returned a few seconds later, bearing a small envelope.

"What's this?" I asked, fumbling with the flap.

Her hand closed in a vise grip around my elbow as she dragged me toward the front door. "Thank you so much for coming by, Eva."

She was throwing me out? But I hadn't even had a chance to show off my continental dining prowess!

"I'm so glad we had this little chat." Her voice was like cold steel.

I finally ripped open the envelope and found . . . *a check made out to me for $150,000?*

"What is this?" I tried to pull away from her, but she was shockingly strong for someone who looked like she was about to crumble into dust.

"Why, Eva, I'm surprised you have to ask." The smile never wavered under her icy glare. "I'm giving you just what I gave your mother—a nice, hefty check to keep your mouth shut and the promise that if you don't, you'll be very sorry indeed."

I thrust the check back at her. "But—"

"Now get out. And this time make sure you stay gone."

As many as 1 in 3 Americans
have HIV and don't know it.

# TAKE CONTROL.
# KNOW YOUR STATUS.
# GET TESTED.

To learn more about HIV testing,
or get a free guide to HIV and
other sexually transmitted diseases.

## www.knowhivaids.org
## 1-866-344-KNOW

09764

# Your attitude. Your style.
# MTV Books:
# Totally your type.